The
KIDDS
of
SUMMERHILL

ANN MURTAGH spent her first seven years in the Bronx, New York. After a short time in Dublin, her family moved to Kells, Co. Meath. She qualified as a primary teacher and later received an MA in Local History from NUI Maynooth. Local history continues to play an important role in her life and she is currently a council member of Kilkenny Archaeological Society. Ann has designed and facilitated history courses for teachers both locally and nationally. She has three sons, Daniel, Bill and Matt, and lives with her husband, Richard, and two dogs in Kilkenny City. She is also the author of *The Sound of Freedom*.

ANN MURTAGH

THE O'BRIEN PRESS
DUBLIN

First published 2021 by The O'Brien Press Ltd,
12 Terenure Road East, Rathgar, Dublin 6, D06 HD27, Ireland.
Tel: +353 1 4923333; Fax: +353 1 4922777
E-mail: books@obrien.ie
Website: www.obrien.ie
The O'Brien Press is a member of Publishing Ireland.

ISBN: 978-1-78849-231-7

Cover illustration: Jon Berkeley
Map: Eoin O'Brien

7 6 5 4 3 2 1
25 24 23 22 21

Printed and bound by Norhaven Paperback A/S, Denmark.
The paper in this book is produced using pulp from managed forests.

The Kidds of Summerhill receives financial assistance from the Arts Council

Published in:

DEDICATION

For Jack and Quinn

ACKNOWLEDGEMENTS

This book was inspired by a visit to 14 Henrietta Street, a social museum of Dublin life. Afterwards I was lucky enough to meet Terry Fagan in the North Inner-City Folklore Project Museum, while it was still open in Railway Street; Terry generously shared his knowledge and experience. I met with similar generosity from Virginia Jennings and her brother Nick Sharkey regarding their family history, and from Roland Doyle, whose mother came from Czechoslovakia. Thanks to the staff of Dublin City Libraries where I accessed Dublin Corporation records for Summerhill and Gloucester Diamond. I would also like to pay tribute to the following: Lucy O'Neill, Nell Galligan and John Coleman for insights into the clothing industry; Kitty McEntee for sharing her nursing experience in the Richmond Hospital; and Helen Madden, archivist for the Mater Hospital, for the time and attention she gave to my queries. Helpful details regarding the Latin Mass were provided by Professor Salvador Ryan and my uncle Oliver Nolan. My thanks to Rebecca Bartlett for feedback on an early draft, and to everyone at The O'Brien Press, especially my editors, Emer Ryan and Nicola Reddy.

The support of my family – Daniel, his wife Lindsay, Bill and Matt – has made writing this book all the more enjoyable. A final thanks to my husband Richard for his honest comments and consistent encouragement.

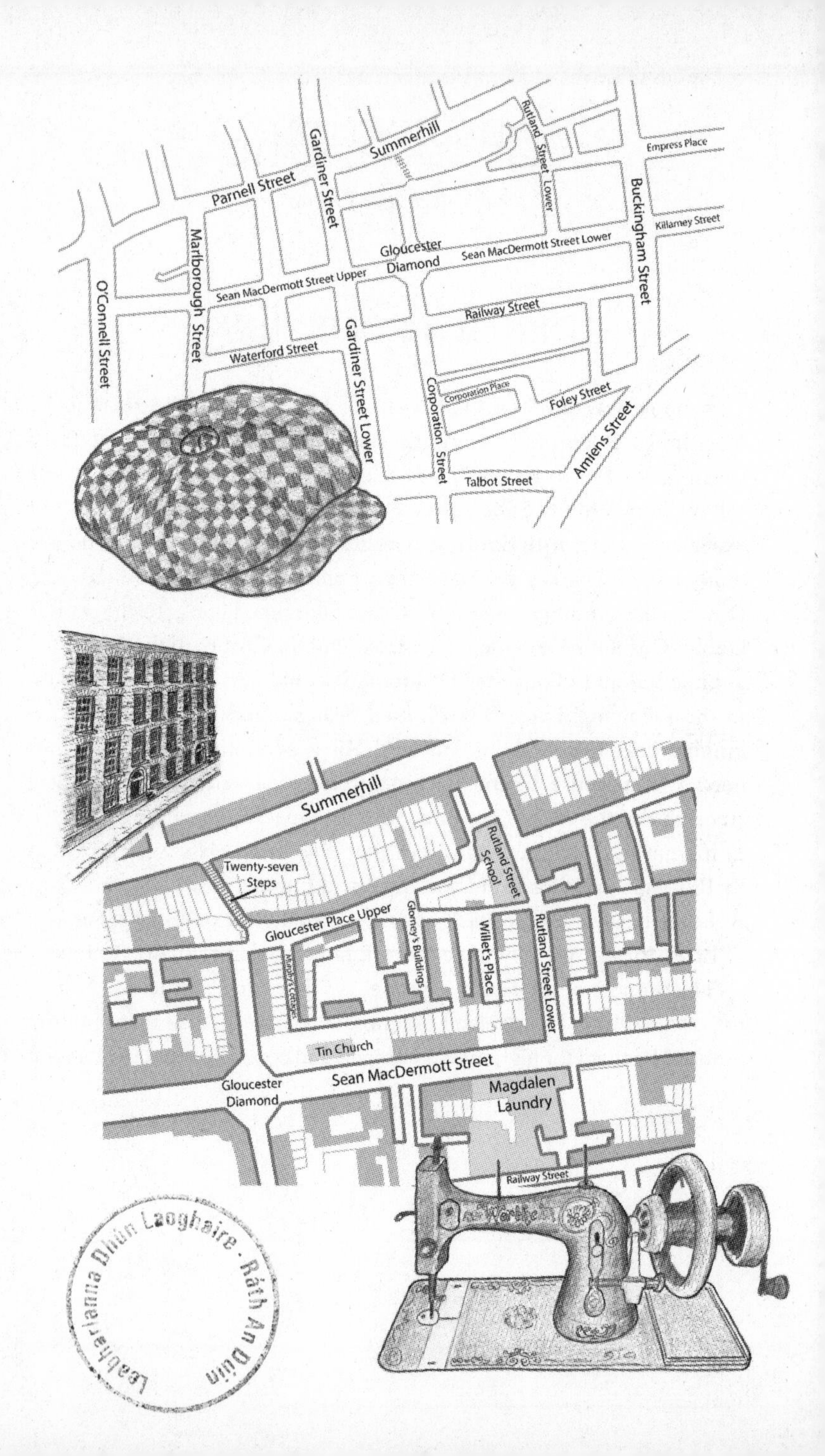
Summerhill
Parnell Street
Gardiner Street
Rutland Street Lower
Empress Place
Buckingham Street
Killarney Street
Marlborough Street
O'Connell Street
Gloucester Diamond
Sean MacDermott Street Upper
Sean MacDermott Street Lower
Railway Street
Waterford Street
Gardiner Street Lower
Corporation Place
Corporation Street
Foley Street
Amiens Street
Talbot Street
Summerhill
Rutland Street School
Twenty-seven Steps
Gloucester Place Upper
Glorney's Buildings
Willet's Place
Rutland Street Lower
Tin Church
Sean MacDermott Street
Gloucester Diamond
Magdalen Laundry
Railway Street

Chapter One

A number eight tram with a sign for 'Denny's Bacon' glided by and ground to a halt. My empty stomach growled. The thought of fried rashers – the smell of them, the taste of them! Sometimes my head felt light when I hadn't eaten. But feeling sorry for myself wasn't going to get me across O'Connell Street safely. You needed your wits about you to weave through the cars, buses and trams, not to mention the horses and carts. Let your guard down and you could end up on the slab in the morgue. And bikes! You couldn't be sure what some people were thinking once they sat up on a saddle. Lilly was always going on about the need for an extra pair of eyes when it came to the bikes.

That Saturday morning in April 1945, we stood at the corner of Henry Street as a wave of black wheeled towards us. Black clothes and black bikes – about a dozen young priests cycled past the GPO and the Pillar. Close behind the last few stragglers, a girl tottered on a rickety old bike, her hair swept under a red felt hat.

'Good afternoon, ladies.'

Lilly linked me. She was wearing long sleeves, but I could feel how thin her arm was.

'Ladies indeed, *Auntie* Mona,' she shouted at the girl as she passed and we both laughed. She was indeed Lilly's aunt, but at fifteen she was only two years older than the pair of us, so Lilly never called her 'Auntie' except when she was trying to take a rise out of her. 'Where are you off to?' she shouted after the red hat but Mona never answered. Probably couldn't hear with the din of Dublin's traffic pounding in her ears.

'Bet it's to a union meeting. That's all we hear about these days,' said Lilly. Mona worked in the Phoenix Laundry in Russell Street and had joined the union after Christmas. She was always going on about workers' rights. We scurried across to the Pillar, the brown paper parcel bought only five minutes earlier squeezed tightly under my arm.

'My ma's looking for the remnant of crêpe de Chine she asked you to put aside,' I had said grandly in Todd, Burns & Co. on Mary Street. Lilly and I watched as the woman in the shop wrapped the blue silky material in brown paper and tied it up neatly with string. It was for Mrs Deegan's blouse, one of Ma's best customers.

Near the entrance to the Pillar, a flower seller held up a bunch of red tulips, the cheeks in her pixie-like face flushed from the warm afternoon.

'You'll not see the likes of these tulips in the four provinces of Ireland,' she shouted to be heard over the traffic. I recognised Mrs Hanlon's voice. Last month she had moved into the basement below us in Summerhill – herself, her husband and their six children. In front of her stood a small woman in a smart navy gabardine coat, rooting for money in her handbag. She pointed to one of the bunches in the pram full of flowers and pressed some coins into Mrs Hanlon's hand. Imagine having money to buy flowers! I watched the woman cross the street clutching a bunch of pink tulips. I wondered who those flowers were for.

'Afternoon, girls,' said a boy's voice, landing me back to the present moment. I stopped short. Mickser Doyle stepped in front of me, blocking my way like a lump of granite. With a grin plastered on his freckled face, he folded his arms, daring me to pass. Nothing gave him more pleasure than to watch our faces to see how we were taking the surprise the pair of them landed on us.

'Not happy to see us?' His pal, Jemmy Nangle, smaller, with the look of a ferret, leaned against the railings of the Pillar. Two lads from the Diamond. I tightened the grip on my parcel.

'Not talkin'?' Mickser asked. I tried to pass, but he side-stepped and blocked me again. He looked down at me with a sneering curl on his lips. I froze.

'We must be invisible, Jemmy,' he said to his friend. In spite of all his bravado, he couldn't hide the tattered jacket or the holes in his boots. I straightened myself up.

'What would we have to say to the likes of you?' I answered. *Show no fear*, I told myself.

'My friend's right,' said Lilly. 'Get out of our way, the pair of yiz. You must be badly stuck for something to do, stoppin' a couple of girls on a Saturday afternoon in the middle of O'Connell Street.'

Lilly had a large forehead and when she held her head back it made her look haughty.

'Meaning what, Miss Hoity Toity?' said Jemmy.

'Meaning get a job and leave us alone,' said Lilly.

Lilly tried to move forward, but Jemmy stood in front of her.

'Get a job! Did you hear what *Miss Lili Marlene* just said, Mickser?'

'Lili Marlene' was a song, but Jemmy made it sound like some sort of curse.

'I did and I feel like bustin' my guts laughing. *Get a job!* As if it was that easy.' He leaned forward and snatched the parcel. My hand shot out to get it back, but he was too fast. He had the parcel thrown to Jemmy as fast as you'd say 'Molly Malone'. Ma's remnant! Lilly pounced on it and started pulling it out of Jemmy's hands. The brown paper started to rip.

'Don't! Don't!' I shouted and she let go. Jemmy threw it back to Mickser.

'Oh, little Nancy Pancy's worried about her parcel,' said Mickser in a sing-song baby voice. He held it above his head to see if I'd jump for it. When I didn't, he threw it over to Jemmy.

'I'm going to call that guard,' I said, nodding to a policeman standing at Laird's Pharmacy across the road from us, 'if you don't give me back my parcel.'

'Ooooooh, I'm really scared.' Jemmy held it over his head again. I could see his hands were filthy and the brown paper had smudges on it. This was an important order for Ma. She had missed a week at work lately, so we were depending on the sewing done at home. Mrs Deegan's blouse could mean dinners for a week. I was about to cross the street towards the guard.

'Never knew Nancy Kidd was a snitch,' said Jemmy. 'Let's—'

The parcel was whipped out of his hand, by somebody behind.

'Oi,' he shouted and turned around.

'Everything all right here, girls?' said a boy standing with newspapers under one arm and the parcel in his free hand. He smiled, showing a tiny gap between his two front teeth.

Jemmy held both his hands up.

'Only having a bit of fun with the girls, Charlie.'

'Fun indeed! He's lying,' said Lilly. 'They wouldn't let us pass.'

'And they took my parcel and wouldn't give it back,' I added.

'Annoying a couple of … respectable girls – taunting them in the street – is this what you call fun?'

Charlie was only fifteen but sounded older.

'Ah here, we were only—' protested Mickser.

'If you boys want to play "pass the parcel", go back to the Diamond and play there,' said Charlie.

'Good one! "Pass the parcel".' Mickser grinned. 'You were always great for a laugh.'

'Nobody's laughing.' Charlie held up the parcel like it was a big fist. 'And if you go near my sister or her friend again, I'll be seeing you in the Diamond and it won't be to play games.' He handed me back Ma's remnant and the two boys skedaddled.

'All right now, girls?' he asked, pulling his cap sideways as he smiled at me. It was a relief to get my parcel back *and* flattering that Charlie had rescued it.

'Thanks,' I said, smiling back. I knew Charlie liked me, but Ma had a thing about newsboys. She was always going on about their roughness and their cheek. When she heard Charlie had taken to selling the papers after his father died, she pressed her lips together and shook her head.

'Charlie's selling the readers? Things must be really bad.' Their ma, Maggie, was a great friend of our ma's.

Another gripe of Ma's was that so many newsboys still ran around in their bare feet when the Herald Boot Fund was handing out free boots. I looked at Charlie's feet and sure enough, he was wearing a pair.

'Admiring my fancy footwear, Miss Kidd?' he said.

'Footwear indeed! I was thinking how lucky we were that you came along,' I lied.

'That's me, Sir Galahad,' he said, grinning. 'I'm heading out towards the Phoenix Laundry to nab the workers coming out at half-twelve.'

'Well, you won't catch Mona,' said Lilly. 'She's after passing us on the bike.'

'Ah no, one of my best customers! Off to join her trade union sisters, no doubt. Sorry, girls. Got to go back to work now.' He turned around and roared. 'Get your *Herald* or *Mail*! Britain closing in on Bremen!'

'Do you have to deafen us?' asked Lilly, putting her hands over her ears.

Charlie ignored her. He spoke to somebody behind us. 'Are you lookin' for a paper, Father?'

A young priest with blond hair was counting change in his hand.

'After seeing Dublin from the Pillar, I might as well find out what's going on in the rest of the world,' he said. He spoke with a funny accent – Cork or Kerry. 'Seeing you're a local lad, could you tell me the best way to get to Killarney Street, please?'

'If you go—'

Charlie stopped. His mouth opened and closed. He pulled the peak of his cap down over his eyes.

'Sorry, Father. Have to run.' He roared at the top of his voice: 'Run!'

A newsboy who had been selling in front of Noblett's Sweet Shop ran towards the GPO. Charlie took off in the opposite direction, racing past the people queuing up for the trams, a long-legged man close on his heels.

'Come back here, ya little blackguard,' the man shouted.

'Oh no,' whispered Lilly. 'It's the Badge Man.'

If a woman pushing a pram hadn't chosen that moment to cross the street, Charlie would have got clean away. But he had to stop and the Badge Man grabbed his arm.

'Who's that man? What's going on?' asked the priest.

Neither of us answered but we ran up the street to where Charlie was trying to pull away. I had never seen the Badge Man up close before. He must have been the tallest man in Dublin. He had a hold of Charlie's arm and was talking in a low voice into his ear.

'Excuse me, sir,' said the priest, panting after running up the street behind us. 'What in heaven's name is going on?'

'Afternoon, Father,' said the Badge Man. 'I'm arresting this vagabond for breaking the law.'

'Breaking what law?'

'Selling newspapers without a licence, Father,' said the Badge Man. 'No badge, you see. No badge, no licence.'

'On whose authority?' asked the priest.

'An Garda Síochána,' said the Badge Man, taking out his own badge from an inside pocket in his coat and showing it to the priest. 'Just doing my job, Father—'

'Father Comiskey,' said the priest. 'A young lad selling a few newspapers – I don't see what all the fuss is about – badge or no badge.'

'Father Comiskey,' said Charlie, 'I haven't got the *money* for a badge – that's why I don't have one. I'm not breakin' the law on purpose.'

The priest and the guard looked at Charlie.

'Well, it's—' started Father Comiskey. A string of curses from the Badge Man stopped him. For a split second he had relaxed his grip on Charlie and Charlie wasn't going to let this chance pass. He was gone, newspapers tucked under his arm, scampering after a bus as it moved off. He grabbed the bar, leapt on board and, swinging around to face us, doffed his cap at us as it sped off.

This was our cue to leave, too. Hang around and the Badge Man would be after *us* for questioning. Lilly took off like a hare down the middle of O'Connell Street and I followed her. The traffic slowed down as cabs pulled up outside the Gresham Hotel. Barely missing a pile of horse dung on the street outside Mackey's Seed Shop, we leaped onto the footpath and turned the corner into Cathal Brugha Street.

'I don't know what we'd do if Charlie got caught,' said Lilly, panting.

The smell of fresh bread from Findlater's bakery teased my empty stomach. Lilly looked over at the mouth-watering rock buns in the window – an old favourite of ours.

'Ma depends on him so much. He's going to sell the papers for another year.'

'And then?

'He'll head over to my uncle in London to work on the buildin's.'

'Why's he waiting?' I asked. 'Surely he'd make better money over there?'

'My uncle said there's a better chance of a decent job for lads over sixteen. Looks like we're stuck with him for another year.'

Another year and then Charlie would be gone. I couldn't imagine Dublin without him. I didn't even want to try. Instead, I linked Lilly as we stepped down Cathal Brugha Street.

'I suppose we'll have to try our best to put up with him,' I said and we grinned at each other.

Chapter Two

I loved those twenty-seven steps that joined Gloucester Diamond to Summerhill. Back in the days when we moved to Dublin first, I'd call down to Lilly in the Diamond to play a game of 'Queenie' or 'Plainy Clappy'. Going back to Summerhill, I used to think the archway at the top of the steps could lead you into another world; like a place where Dorothy might have gone in *The Wizard of Oz*. Mrs Gaynor, who sold fish out of her pram under the archway on Fridays, was like the magic keeper of that world and I used to pretend that she wouldn't let me pass unless I knew a magic password. Now that I was in Sixth Class, the daydreaming was over but I knew that once I passed through the archway, I was almost home.

That Monday afternoon, my sister Kate and I were perched on the third last step. Kate was in Fifth Class. Like me, she wore her long black hair in two plaits. Our school bags were thrown on the step below us.

At the bottom of the steps, the footpath was Lilly's stage and we were her audience. Lucky for us, she had been to see a film the night before. Mona had called for her and brought her to the cinema in Mary Street. She felt sorry for Lilly who hadn't been to the pictures in months. They were showing *The*

Keys of the Kingdom. Lilly could tell you about a film in a way that you could see the whole thing happening in your head. We may have been on 'the steps' in the middle of Dublin, but in our minds, we were in a place called Tweedside in Scotland. Lilly was warming to the story now.

'Black dark outside, it is, and the rain's bucketing down out of the heavens. The da's in town on business. He knows there might be trouble, but nothing's going to stop him going home. Mind you, with the rain hammering down on him and the wind blasting against him, he can hardly walk along the road. Suddenly, somebody sneaks up behind him – three lads with big sticks – clubs, I think you'd call them. And one of them says, "There's that dirty papist."'

Lilly did a good Scottish accent. I drew in my breath.

'What's a papist?'

'Do you know nothing, Nancy?' said Kate. 'It's a fancy word for a Catholic. Go on, Lilly. What happened next?'

Lilly paused and tilted her head slightly – a signal to us that the pause was for a good reason and we were not to look around. Somebody was coming down the steps behind us. Somebody moving slowly and wheezing loudly. A walking stick clicked like the teacher's metronome in school. A smell of pigs filled the air. We froze on the steps, willing the person to pass us by as quickly as possible.

'Time there was when respectable people could walk down

these steps and not have to step aside for the likes of you,' snorted the Pig Farmer, her pink fleshy face turned away. She never looked at us when she spoke.

Everyone knew that you could fit a Johnston Mooney & O'Brien van down those steps, but we knew better than to say this to the Pig Farmer. Instead, we sat completely still. We were used to this. Every time she met us in the hallway of the house we were unlucky enough to share with her, we pretended we didn't see her, as this is what *she* always did to us – unless she saw a chance to throw a nasty comment our way.

Squeezed into her long man's coat, the colour of porridge, she hobbled down the last couple of steps. People said that old coat belonged to her husband, Martin, but Ma said it couldn't be that old as he was dead this thirty years. She paused for a moment on the last step, then shuffled off to the left towards Glorney's Buildings. I stood up and did a mock curtsey after her.

'Time there was that you could sit on these steps without being given out to by an auld one,' I said in that same nasal voice.

The Pig Farmer turned around. I thought she was too far ahead to have heard me, but she had her lower lip pushed out as she made her way back towards the steps. I was getting ready for a dressing down, when she suddenly veered towards Murphy's Cottages.

'What on earth is she up to?' asked Kate.

'Shush! She's in with all the Cruelty Men,' whispered Lilly. 'Don't go upsetting her.'

Lilly's da had died a year ago and her ma, Maggie, lived in dread of the Society for the Prevention of Cruelty to Children. We called them 'the Cruelty Men' for short. She was sure they were watching her all the time. They could pounce on her for not being a good enough ma, and take her children off her. It was hard for us to imagine anyone would think big-hearted Maggie wasn't a good ma.

'Never mind the Pig Farmer. Tell us more about the film,' said Kate.

'You were at the part where those men are followin' the da?' I reminded Lilly.

'That's right, and mean-looking gurriers they are too, like those boyos in the animal gangs, only they're not from Dublin and they hate Catholics. They beat the lard out of the poor man and leave him for dead on the side of the road.'

'But is he dead?' asked Kate.

'He isn't. But while this is going on, the wife at home gets fed up waiting. Out she goes looking for him—'

'And what about Francis?' I asked. This was their son. Lilly had mentioned him earlier, and instead of Roddy McDowall playing the part, I imagined Charlie. His handsome face would look so well on the screen.

'Well, *he's* not sticking around at home. He says goodbye to his pretty cousin – pretty *distant* cousin – and off he goes after the mother.' I had myself playing the role of the distant cousin.

'On his way into town, he has to cross a river. The storm has it flowing like a mad yoke and the footbridge across it is in bits. What do you think our boy Francis sees?'

We both shrugged our shoulders.

'His ma and da trying to cross the bridge and the river pulling them in.'

Kate swallowed. 'What happens next?'

'The bridge collapses and the two of them drown in front of Francis's eyes.' She paused to see how we were taking it. Her cheeks had turned red now; they always did with the excitement of telling a story.

'Does Francis come safe?' I asked.

'Indeed, he does … Ah no! Watch out, Nancy!'

I felt my plait being pulled and turned around. Charlie stood inches away, grinning beneath his newsboy cap, as usual worn sideways. I tried not to, but I blushed. What would he say if he knew he was the boy in the film running in my head seconds ago? I let on I was cross.

'Mind whose hair you're pullin'!'

'How are the Miss Kidds?' said Charlie, tipping his cap and sitting on the step behind us. 'Sorry to interrupt, Sis. I'm happy enough to enjoy the show from the cheap seats back here.'

'What about your newspapers? Selling themselves, are they?'

'I've a few free minutes and thought I'd catch a good outdoor show. I knew there'd be one on the steps this afternoon since Mona managed to tear herself away from her trade union pals to bring you to the pictures last night.' He grinned at us. 'After that, I'm off down to Prince's Street to collect the *Heralds*.' He jingled some coins in his pocket. 'I'll be selling in Amiens Street this evening – working my way down to the station.'

'Why don't you take the train while you're at it and give me a chance to finish my story?' said Lilly. 'I'm still stuck in the year 1878.'

'That's all right, Elizabeth,' he said, giving Lilly her proper name. 'I won't stay where I'm not wanted.' Toes turned out, holding the papers under one arm and an imaginary cane in the other, he shuffled up the steps like Charlie Chaplin. Kate and I giggled. Even Lilly had to laugh.

'Go on with you, Charlie Chaplin, and leave us alone.'

He swaggered off.

'Oh brother, here's another one,' said Lilly, looking behind us.

Halfway down the steps, my eight-year-old brother, Patrick, had been running that fast he was hardly able to talk.

'Ma said you and Kate have to come home this minute.'

'Ma's home?' I asked. She worked in Robilon's and normally wouldn't be home until five.

'She's home since twelve o'clock,' said Patrick. 'She got sick at work.'

We both jumped up. When Ma was at work, she never left early.

'I'd better run to Kennedy's to get the bread,' said Kate. 'I've the pillowcase in my bag.' Kennedy's in Parnell Street sold yesterday's bread or 'fancy bread' at a good price, and a pillowcase was a handy way to carry it home.

'Come over to me in the yard at school tomorrow and I'll finish the story,' said Lilly. 'Hope your ma'll be all right, girls.'

She snatched her bag and wove through the girls playing 'All in Together' with their skipping rope. Patrick took off to his friend Brendan's house, in Sean MacDermott Street, with a warning from me about when to come home. Kate had disappeared through the archway on her way to Parnell Street. I picked up my bag and rushed up the rest of the steps to the sound of the girls' chant:

All in together, girls

This fine weather, girls.

Chapter Three

Ma was propped up in bed by a bunch of old clothes; that was to help her breathe, but you could still hear the rattle in her chest. Granny's white crochet bedspread was pulled up to her chin. The shutters on the two windows were closed, and only for the faint light from the embers in the fire, the room would have been in complete darkness. It was a matter of pride to her that our room – the back parlour – not only had two windows but they were the only ones – along with the Pig Farmer's – whose shutters hadn't been burned for fuel.

'Good girl, Nance,' she said.

'Hiya, Ma. Patrick told me you were home. Are y'all right?'

'The cough … Couldn't stay.'

My eyes were getting used to the dim light. Ma's flushed cheeks made her lips look pale. She coughed into a hankie held in her fist, trying to hide the spots of blood.

'Let me get you a cup of water,' I said, wanting to run from the room as another bout of coughing started. I took her cup from the dresser – she had been told to have her own cup and plate on account of the sickness – and scooped some water out of the bucket. She held the cup with both hands as she took a long drink. The blood-stained hankie was nowhere to be seen. What could I say to make her feel better?

'I see you've got two letters,' I said, pointing to the envelopes beside her pillow. She held up one.

'One from Aunt Gretta.'

Gretta was Ma's aunt. She lived in Leeds – a city we had called home until the war broke out in 1939. To keep us safe, Ma brought us back to Dublin in September that year, but we had always planned on going back, once the war was over.

'Any news?'

'The usual. Her friend Mimi is still at her to move up to Whitby.'

'Doesn't Mimi know that we're moving back?'

'She does, but—'

'But what, Ma?'

'To tell you the truth, Nance, I don't think I'm able for the journey.'

I felt a twinge in my stomach. Not able for the journey back to Leeds! This was the first time she had said anything about not being able to go.

'Look, the second letter here is from the doctor. I finally got a bed in the Pigeon House. After some treatment, I might feel more up to going.'

The Pigeon House Hospital in Ringsend was for people with consumption.

'That's great, Ma,' I said, hoping I sounded happier than I felt inside. Many a neighbour had gone to the Pigeon House to the last bed they ever lay in. 'I'll take the day off school and go with you.'

'No, love. I've it all arranged with Maggie. She was over here this afternoon as soon as word got around that I was home.'

'What do you mean "word got around"?'

'Your old ma arrived at her *residence* in style, you see,' she said, her voice a little stronger. 'The boss – Mr O'Toole, himself – had his own doctor drive me home. Said it was a medical emergency. You should have seen the women when we drove down Summerhill. Some of them nearly fell out the windows when they saw the big swanky car and me getting out of it.'

She stopped to cough, then continued:

'Maggie wasn't working today and as soon as she heard about it, she was around in a flash. She's going to go on the later shift tomorrow so she can bring me over to Ringsend.'

'What about Mrs Deegan's blouse?' I asked.

'It's almost finished,' she said. 'Will you hem it? I have it pinned. I promised Mrs Deegan she'd get it back tomorrow.'

'I'll finish it this evening and deliver it after school tomorrow.'

'In the meantime, I'm going to ask you to take charge of things here. You don't mind, love?'

'Of course not, Ma.'

'The books for the rent, the rations, the children's allowance and the pension are in the biscuit tin under the bed.' Ma had a British Army pension since Da was killed in Egypt three years before.

'Where's Kate?'

'Gone to buy some fancy bread in Kennedy's. She'll be home shortly. It's her turn to cook the dinner. Will you try a bit, Ma?'

'Later. I'll have some later. Are the lads home yet?'

'No. Patrick's called over to Brendan's. I told him to come home as soon as he sees the Rag and Bone man on his way to Corporation Street. I haven't seen Tom since this mornin'.'

'I'll close my eyes now. Hardly slept last night, I was sweatin' that much. You can leave me be for a bit, Nance.'

I closed the door quietly.

★ ★ ★

Kate held an open book in one hand and Ma's old ladle in the other. Every so often, she'd stir the mutton soup in the saucepan and then stick her nose back into her book. I took out four bowls from the cupboard and set them on the table. A snore came from Ma's room, so I knew it was safe to talk.

'Ma's going into the Pigeon House tomorrow.'

Kate closed the book and gave the soup another stir.

'The cough's been so bad—' she whispered.

'I know none of us wants her there, but we don't want to see her suffer either.'

'It's just—' Kate left down the ladle and took up the poker, to give the turf and sticks under the pot a good poke.

'I know what you're thinking but she needs to be in a place where she can be properly looked after. And Ma won't be our only worry.'

Kate turned around to me.

'There'll be no money coming in from Robilon's,' I said quietly.

'At least we have Da's pension.'

'True, but we won't get by on that.'

Kate pointed the ladle at a statue of the Virgin Mary on the mantelpiece. 'I can't understand why Ma won't pawn *her* or some of the other holy statues of Granny's. What about that picture of the Sacred Heart?' This was the picture of Jesus pointing to his heart that had a crown of thorns around it and a little flame over it. 'That'd get a nice few shillin's.'

'Sshh! Keep your voice down,' I whispered. Between the kitchen and Ma's room there was only a wooden partition that went three-quarters of the way up the wall. 'You know quite well why she won't. She takes pride in the fact that we never had to pawn any of the holy things, *plus* they all belonged to Granny. She's sentimental about them.'

'Being sentimental won't put food on the table,' said Kate, adding a little more salt to the soup. 'And I'm sure Granny wouldn't want us to go hungry for the sake of a few holy statues.'

I smiled. Honora Murphy, our granny, *was* a practical woman, but like Ma she had been a proud one too.

I straightened the statue on the mantelpiece. It had been there since Ma was a little girl. So had that picture of the Sacred Heart and the statue of the Child of Prague with Granny's mother-of-pearl rosary beads strung around him.

Kate had opened the window on account of the warm evening, but the smell of the piggery out the back was worse than usual. I could hear the Pig Farmer throwing the slops into the troughs. I pulled down the sash, but it was always stiff and closed with a bang.

'What about asking Tom to sell newspapers?' suggested Kate.

'Ma would have a fit if she thought we were even talking about it,' I said.

'If she's away, how is she to know? You could ask Charlie to show him the ropes. I'm sure he'd be pleased to oblige.'

I felt a blush making its way into my cheeks.

'Don't say anything to Tom. Let me handle it.'

The sound of hobnailed boots in the hall was followed by Tom and Patrick bursting into the kitchen.

'Shhh. Ma's in bed.'

'I'm starving. Give us a good bowl of mutton soup,' said Tom, sitting down at the table.

'We're all starving, Tom,' Kate told him. 'There's lots of fancy bread if you're that hungry. But for goodness sake, will you go and wash yourself? You've brought half the muck of the street in with you.'

If Tom's face was anything to go by, she was right. There were dirty smears across his cheeks. His mouth went into a pout, like Da's used to do. He also had Da's dark eyes and followed the Kidd side of the family when it came to being tall. At ten years of age he was the same height as Kate. Patrick, on the other hand, took after Ma's side. Although he was eight, he'd have passed for six.

'How was school today, Patrick?' I asked.

'All right, but two lads were teasing me because Da came from England,' he said.

'Who?' asked Tom.

'Joe O'Dea and Tim Benson,' said Patrick, stuffing some bread into his mouth.

'What did they say?'

'The teacher was talking about Hitler and all the bad things he was doing and I told the class that Da died fighting the Germans. Joe said he couldn't have because his da is in the Irish army and they didn't fight in the war. Then I told him

Da came from England and he had joined the British Army. As soon as we were let out for break, they followed me in the yard, calling me a Brit.'

'Did you not tell the teacher?' asked Kate.

'And be called a tell-tale? No, I didn't! And they were calling Brendan a Brit too, even though his da is from Sean MacDermott Street.'

Brendan's father was also in the British Army.

'Never mind that pair of gits,' said Tom. 'I'll hang 'round tomorrow and make sure they won't be after you again.' He grabbed a bar of soap and a towel to wash at the tap in the yard.

Once Tom was back, I poured the soup into bowls.

'Listen,' I began, 'we got some news from Ma today. She's a place in the Pigeon House.'

Tom looked down at the table.

'When is she going?'

'Tomorrow,' I said.

'Can children go to it?' asked Patrick.

'Of course,' I said. 'We can go to see her on Sunday.'

'Wasn't that where Mrs Tumulty went last year?' asked Patrick.

'That's right,' I said slowly, dreading what he was going to ask me next.

'Didn't she die there?'

I took a spoonful of soup. 'She did, and—'

I stirred the soup in my bowl, trying to think of something to say to take the sting out of Mrs Tumulty's death.

'She must have been much worse than Ma to go and die like that, isn't that right, Nancy?' said Patrick.

I was spared having to reply to this by a knock on the door. Kate opened it and stepped out into the hallway. She came back inside, opened the pillowcase on the sideboard and took out a piece of bread. Snatching a knife off the table, she spread some dripping on it. Before I got a chance to say anything, she was back in the hallway again. There was a short murmur of voices. She closed the door and slipped back into her place at the table.

'That was Sconsie,' she said. 'He heard Ma wasn't well and asked how she was. I knew he was in a bad way for a bit of food, so—'

'You handed him out some of ours. For heaven's sake, Kate, you shouldn't be encouraging him,' I told her. 'Askin' about Ma indeed. More like he was on the touch for a bit of bread.'

'And doesn't he have to eat the same as the rest of us?' said Kate.

'If he spent less time in those pubs along the quays, he'd have more money for food,' I said. 'No wonder the stairways are filthy with the likes of him sleeping there. You shouldn't be drawing him or any other knockabout into the house, handin' out bread and the likes.'

'A bit of bread – I don't see what all the fuss is about,' said Tom.

'He always says "hello" and calls me "the little master",' said Patrick. 'I don't care what you say, Nancy. I like him.'

'Well, little master, I'm going to open a window. I'm nearly dead with the heat in here,' said Tom. He opened the window and the stench from the piggery wafted in. 'God, Éamon and Seán are at their finest this evening.'

It was well known that Martin Knaggs, the Pig Farmer's husband, had fought and died in the First World War. The Pig Farmer never forgave the leaders of the 1916 Rising – Éamon de Valera among them – for destroying Dublin 'and murderin' decent people' when 'her Martin' lost his life in Flanders. From then on, she badmouthed 'that Dev fella'. After he formed Fianna Fáil she always named the oldest pigs after himself and Seán Lemass.

'I heard the Corpo's trying to close her down, but she won't budge unless she gets the right price.'

'Who told you that?' I asked.

'Spud heard the Pig Farmer telling his granny. They're both in the Legion of Mary.'

'It'd be great if it *was* closed. The smell of them this evening would turn your stomach,' I said.

'He heard her talkin' about Maggie, too,' said Tom.

'Maggie?' I said. 'What did she say?'

'The Cruelty Men are watching her.'

'And?'

'They said they are very *concerned* – yes, that was the word – about the Weavers since Lar died.'

Lar was Lilly's da.

'What else did they say?' I asked.

'They were going on about Charlie. Maggie's getting him to sell newspapers, but won't buy him a badge.'

'Hasn't the Pig Farmer little to do talking about the Weavers like that?' I said. 'She thinks she's a great woman with all her craw-thumping and all her trotting up and down to the Tin Church, but she doesn't behave like a Christian around *us*.'

The Tin Church was the little chapel in Sean MacDermott Street, made out of corrugated iron.

'I like the way *Maggie* behaves,' said Patrick. 'Specially the way she's like an auntie to us. The Pig Farmer's more like the witch in *The Wizard of Oz*.'

'The Cruelty Men don't see it like that,' I said.

'She was going on about Lilly, too,' said Tom. 'The way she's always missin' school to look after Imelda and the twins.' Imelda was five and the twins, Mary and Breda, were three. 'She talked about the two boys, too.'

'What?' I said. 'About Raymie and Larry?'

'Yes. She said if they were at home with their ma and da

instead of being minded by their uncle that night, they'd both be alive today.'

'Oh, she's, she's—' I felt so cross, I couldn't think of the right word.

'Cruel is what I'd call it,' said Kate. 'Imagine blaming Maggie for leaving Raymie and Larry with her brother for *one* night? I don't remember the Pig Farmer offering to look after the boys when Maggie had to rush the twins to hospital.'

'I suppose it was Maggie's fault too that the house collapsed,' I said.

'Are you going to say anything to Lilly?' asked Kate.

'No. They know they're being watched, so I don't see how it'd help them. That old Pig Farmer. I wish she'd keep her snout in her own business.'

'You know when that'll happen?' asked Tom.

We all answered in a chorus.

'When pigs will fly.'

Chapter Four

The school bell rang on the dot of three. No dilly-dallying for me today as I jostled for a place among the first batch of girls in the stampede out the school gate. Among the books and copies in my bag was Mrs Deegan's blouse, wrapped in a sheet of clean brown paper Ma had in the dresser. I made my way to Gardiner Place and knocked on the big brass knocker – once, as Ma had told me to do. I was standing, holding the parcel, when a girl in a white blouse with a silver fáinne brooch pinned at the collar opened the door, took one look at me and was gone before I opened my mouth.

'Your parcel's here, Aunt Maude.'

A grey-haired woman in a light blue dress covered by a navy apron appeared at the door. I recognised the dress; Ma had made it last year. The woman looked at me as if I had come to the wrong person, to the wrong house, with the wrong parcel.

'I was expecting your mother,' she said, fishing for money in her apron. Holding the coins in her fist, she dropped them into my open hand. 'There's the correct amount.' Mrs Deegan always paid straight away and that's why Ma liked doing work for her. When the parcel was taken and the door banged, I turned to go home.

I put the money into my school bag and dawdled along the footpath. I was in no hurry home. It would be the first day when Ma didn't arrive in after work, take off her hat and say 'hello' to us before hanging her coat on the peg on the back of the door. She wasn't going to be there to ask about school, who we talked to, who we played with, who was in trouble with the teacher, who was missing. I wanted the first evening to be over: the first time of not seeing Ma in her chair at the fire, or at the table, her head bent over her sewing machine. And I wanted the time to go fast until visiting hour on Sunday in the Pigeon House.

Kate was gone to the library. Tom was playing a game of pitch and toss with his friends. Patrick was probably playing with Brendan. The usual group of women stood on the steps of the house in Summerhill. Mrs Boland, who lived in the 'two pair back', always claimed the top step, her shawl pulled tightly around her. Two other women, also in shawls, heads almost touching, stood with their backs to me. Mrs McGee, from the back drawing-room, rocked back and forth, soothing little Jack in her arms. Ma always referred to her as 'Busybody McGee'. Mrs Perrin, her neighbour, stood beside her. As soon as Mrs Boland spotted me, she gave a quick nod to the others that I was coming. The chat came to a full stop.

'Ah, would ya look at the poor lamb now,' said Mrs McGee, patting the baby's back. 'Maggie's in there waiting for you.'

I wouldn't give her the satisfaction of asking her for what, especially in front of the others, but I wondered at the sorrowful tone of her voice and the fact that she called me 'lamb'.

Sconsie sat hunched on the third step. He took off his cap but kept staring at the floor.

'The decent woman. The decent woman,' he mumbled.

I had a feeling Ma mightn't have gone, maybe was too sick to move and was still in bed inside. I pushed the door open and ran in. Maggie was sitting at the table. She had her good frock on – the one that Lilly told me she had to get taken in because she was so much thinner now than the day she bought it in the Daisy Market. Her fair hair was brought back into a bun and she had freckles on her nose from the few days of sunshine. Before I got a chance to speak, Kate and Patrick burst in the door.

'Lilly told us we were wanted at home,' said Kate. She stopped when she saw Ma's dark red carpet-bag – the one she brought from Leeds – sitting on the table. Maggie stood up and ushered us to the chairs at the table.

Tom opened the door.

'Where's Ma?' he panted.

'Sit down, all of yiz,' said Maggie and she patted Ma's bag. She gave us a few seconds to pull in our chairs, but she stayed standing.

'Has something happened?' I asked.

'It has, love. I'm going to tell you now.' She swallowed. She scratched the back of her neck. I had seen her do that before when she was trying to think of what to say. 'Your ma and I were headin' to the Pigeon House this morning. We had to get the bus for Ringsend. The pair of us were walking along the footpath. I was takin' my time on account of her finding it hard to catch her breath.'

Out on the street, a dog started barking. A man's voice from upstairs shouted at it to stop.

'Out of breath she was, and what happened only the poor woman collapsed, and us goin' up Marlborough Street.'

'Collapsed? Where is she now?'

'Let me finish, Nancy. We were passin' that eating house up from the Pro-Cathedral – you know the one next to the priests' house – when the poor darlin' fell over, banging her head off the wall below the railings. I'll never forget it, blood everywhere. Mr Henry, the owner, was very good. Called the ambulance and got her taken to the Richmond Hospital.'

'So, she's in the Richmond?' I said.

'She is and … she never opened her eyes after, never said a word.'

Kate grabbed Maggie's hand.

'Never opened her eyes?'

'Is she…?' I asked.

'She is, darlin',' said Maggie, her bottom lip quivering.

'Is what?' asked Patrick.

'She's left us, little man,' said Maggie softly. 'She wasn't well and that bang on her head finished her. She died before she got to the hospital.'

She started sobbing. We all sat looking at her, trying to take in what we were hearing; hoping it wasn't true, but knowing full well that it was. My heart felt like it was being squeezed by a big pincers. Tom broke the silence first.

'What are we going to do without her?' he said over and over between his choking sobs. Maggie put her arm around him. I put my arms around Patrick, and Kate put her arms around the two of us, and it felt as if we were all one person, crying for our ma from our hearts – from what Lilly would call our 'deepest hearts'.

'Can we go and see her?' I asked. Maggie paused and blew her nose with her hankie.

'Seeing you're the oldest, I think that you should come to the hospital with me and we'll arrange for her to be brought home.'

Ma to be brought home. Not to talk to or laugh with or listen to. We were bringing her home to say goodbye.

'Tom, run up to the Parochial House and let Fr Gill know,' said Maggie. 'He'll be sorry, I can tell you. He was fond of your mother, and indeed your granny, Lord rest them both. Kate and Patrick, you have to honour your ma by getting the rooms here spick and span.'

Kate put her arm around Patrick.

'We're the right people for that job,' said Kate, trying to keep from crying again. 'Patrick is the best duster in Summerhill.'

Before I left, I snatched the red carpet-bag up from the table and kicked it under Ma's bed. I followed Maggie out the door as if I was walking in a dream.

* * *

A nurse in a crisp white uniform, starched within an inch of its life, looked coldly at Maggie as we crossed the hallway, but when she heard us ask for the morgue, her face softened and she insisted on bringing us there herself.

'What was the poor woman's name?' she asked Maggie.

'Esther Kidd.'

We were brought into a room with shiny green tiles on the wall. Ma lay on a slab, the cut on the side of her forehead all cleaned up. I couldn't believe how thin she had become. How did I not notice before? Her hair brushed back off her face was down around her shoulders instead of in the usual bun. It made her look girlish. I patted it. Maggie had her big white hankie out again, dabbing her eyes.

'There's the truest friend I ever had,' she said. 'I remember when she left Dublin to work as a housekeeper in Leeds.

Esther Murphy she was then and not much older than you are now. It went hard on the pair of us to be separated. But she had her Aunt Gretta to train her in a good job, and wasn't she right to go?'

'She got a letter from Aunt Gretta yesterday.'

'Still on for yiz all to move back?'

'Yes, she is, or at least she was while Ma was still … with us.'

'She'll be sending for yiz now, you can be sure. And isn't your da's family over there too?'

Da's family weren't great letter writers; we had lost touch as the years went by.

'That's right.'

We both stood, staring at Ma.

'Yes, she'd want you to go ahead with the plans for Leeds. And you're the right girl to look after the others. I always said to your ma that you're a brave girl and one that could always stick up for herself.' Maggie's eyes filled up with tears. She put her arm around me.

'I always admired you for it.' She squeezed my shoulder until she had to let go to wipe her eyes and her nose. 'Your ma there would have had every faith in you to look after the others until you go to Leeds. At least you remember living there, Nancy. It won't be like going to a strange country.'

I *did* remember Leeds, especially moving into the Quarry Hill flats the year before we moved to Ireland. It felt like we were millionaires. When we had to leave and come to Dublin, it was a big change.

'Your ma was sad to leave it,' said Maggie. 'But with all the bombing going on … she did the right thing. I remember your granny coming over to tell me that you'd all be arrivin' the following week. She was thrilled with the news. To think that she died with galloping consumption a year later. And your ma to be struck down with it as well. The poor unfortunates.'

Maggie took up one of Ma's hands and rubbed it. 'She had terrific hands. There wasn't a garment she couldn't make. You've been blessed the same way.'

For a few moments, the room was so quiet I could hear myself breathe.

'Nancy, while you're still in Dublin – don't ever forget – if you need someone, I'm here,' said Maggie quietly.

So much to take in. Ma lying on the slab, Maggie whispering beside me.

Footsteps and voices outside disturbed the quiet moment in the morgue. The door opened and a man entered, his arm outstretched. He took Maggie's hand and shook it.

'Hello,' he said. 'Fr Gill is giving the last rites to a woman in the parish and he couldn't come to the hospital.'

'You must be the new priest?' said Maggie.

'I am. Was Esther Kidd your sister?' he asked.

'No. She didn't have a sister, nor a brother for that matter.'

'But had she family?'

'Four children. Nancy here is her eldest.'

The light was dim in the morgue but when he came closer, I recognised him.

'I met you … Fr Comiskey?'

'Of course ... at the Pillar,' he said. 'I'm sorry about your mother. She had consumption, the nurse was telling me.'

I nodded.

'And you're … what age?'

'Fourteen in June,' I said.

'The same age I was when my mother died. Such a hard time. You've to go through it to know what it's really like. No doubt you've got a good friend in Maggie here.'

'Her mother and myself were friends since we were in school together,' said Maggie, putting her arm around my shoulder. She stopped. A gong sounded in the distance. Fr Comiskey closed his eyes and counted the beats in whispers.

'That's to tell us that Mr Bellew has entered the building. He's one of the surgeons. You'll have to excuse me – I have to see him about a patient. Hope you'll be all right, Nancy. I'll call on you before the funeral.'

★ ★ ★

'Where did your ma keep the empty sugar bags?'

I went back into the kitchen and rooted in the first drawer

of the dresser. Handing one to Maggie, I knew what would follow. She'd send it upstairs to Mrs McGee. A few coins would be added before it would be passed on to next door. After Mrs Perrin added money, she'd bring it up to Mr Evans in the two pair front on the next floor. He'd pass it on to Bolands in the two pair back. Mrs Boland would bring it up to the top floor. Nobody ever asked the Pig Farmer for a donation, but you could be sure that once it finished in our house it would go around a couple of the shops. The money collected would help pay for Ma's funeral.

Maggie was writing out the words to be sent by telegram to Aunt Gretta.

'Off you go, Kate. You've the money and the note.'

'Right, I want you to go and get a handywoman, Nancy. Someone to do a good job of getting your ma ready for the wake. Go for Aggie McPartland in Railway Street; she's the best one. Tom, could you get one of your ma's fuel vouchers and head to the depot to get us some turf for the fire? Lilly, I need you to go back to our house and knock on Mrs Casey's next door and ask her to keep an eye on the girls for another while. Tell her I'll be back before teatime. Patrick, I'll need someone to help me here, so you're going to stay with me.'

Chapter Five

Aggie, the handywoman, beckoned us in. I tiptoed through the kitchen like I was afraid to wake Ma up. The others crept behind me. Patrick held on to the back of my jumper as we went past the fireplace. Ma would have been proud of the roaring fire in the grate.

There was a strong smell of disinfectant. Maggie had sent Kate down earlier to Con Foley's to get some flea powder so that the hoppers wouldn't be annoying the people coming to the wake. The bed had been moved out to the kitchen, where it now stood in a corner. Ma lay, decked out in a white satin shroud, with a patchwork quilt in a rainbow of colours draped over her. Her fingers were clasped around a cross that was sticking up, and Granny's mother-of-pearl rosary beads were woven through them. Behind her, a white sheet pinned to the wallpaper had a cross made of black crêpe in the middle of it. Another sheet pinned to the ceiling made a kind of canopy over her.

Her eyes were closed. I thought about all the nights her cough had kept her awake – how she'd be desperate for a good night's sleep – and now here she was the picture of peace. Patrick buried his face in the cover of the bed and sobbed. Kate rubbed his back, crying behind him. I leaned over and kissed Ma's cheek. The smell of Sunlight soap was still on it, though it was as cold as any of those Holy Mary statues that we'd talked about pawning. I pushed a few stray ribs of hair behind her ear. She'd be delighted if she could see how well she was looking for the neighbours.

★ ★ ★

'Poor Esther. Wouldn't you know she's gone straight to Heaven by the face of her,' said Mrs McGee. 'Nobody can turn a corpse out like Aggie McPartland.'

'And the two daughters,' added Mrs Perrin. She took the white feather from the kitchen table and dipped it into the holy water and sprinkled Ma. You'd think she was the Queen of Sheba the way she did it.

'The Lord have mercy on you,' she said. I had to bite back a laugh that was starting in my throat. Ma couldn't stand the guts of Mrs Perrin and here she was being blessed by her, in her own home too.

'Is Gretta coming home from Leeds for the funeral?' Mrs McGee asked. I knew it wouldn't be long before the questions would start.

'She can't, Mrs McGee. She has bad arthritis in her hip and wasn't able to make the journey.'

'Of course, she was ten years older than Honora,' said Mrs McGee. 'Did she send yiz money to help with the funeral?'

'Will you stop annoyin' the girl with questions?' said Mrs Perrin.

'I was only askin',' said Mrs McGee, a little huff in her voice.

★ ★ ★

It was the third night of the wake and there was hardly breathing space in the kitchen with all the neighbours in. The door out to the hall was open; there were as many outside as there were in the room. Sconsie held court on the stairs.

One end of the table was like a mountain of sandwiches, minerals and bottles of stout. At the other end, Ma's tea set was laid out and Mrs McGee was pouring tea for the women as they discussed what game would be played next.

'The night's stretchin' ahead of us,' said Mrs Perrin. 'And there's nothing like a game of "Forfeits" to make the time go fast. Did you hear about Dixie McArdle's wake in number 11 there a couple of weeks ago?'

'Didn't hear anything out of the ordinary,' said Mrs McGee.

'Well, someone dared my sister Dolly to get a tram ticket with number 608 at Nelson's Pillar and bring it back. The poor girl searched the streets and footpaths around your man, found loads of tickets, but not one of them had the right number.'

'What did she have to do as a forfeit?'

Mrs McGee started giggling.

'You know that stout woman that lives with her sister at the top of that house? Well, a pair of her bloomers were hangin' on the clothesline downstairs. What did my sister have to do only empty all the straw out of a mattress in the house, pin the bottom of the legs on the bloomers and stuff them with the straw? That was how the poor woman found them the next morning. She didn't know whether to laugh or cry when she saw them.'

'Imagine if we did that to a pair of the Pig Farmer's drawers,' whispered Mrs McGee. Mrs Perrin covered her mouth with her hand and giggled.

Mrs McGee gave her a playful tap on the arm and cleared her throat. 'So, everybody, are we on for a game of "Forfeits"?'

All those in the room said they were.

'All right, I'll start. This is for you, Mrs Hanlon. I dare you … to write on a piece of paper "I love De Valera" and nail it to the Pig Farmer's door.'

There was laughter all around at this.

'Wait a minute!' said Mrs Perrin. 'Michael has a few Fianna Fáil election posters left from last year. What if I nipped up and got one of those instead? That'd really get her goin'!'

Everyone thought this was a great idea. Maggie, Lilly and

Charlie were on their way in, and Mrs Perrin stopped for a minute to chat to Maggie before heading upstairs for the poster. Charlie moved towards me and squeezed my hand.

'Doin' all right?' he asked kindly.

'Doin' well enough,' I answered. I didn't tell him I was heartbroken, exhausted, and worried about the future. Instead, I explained about the game. Mrs Perrin arrived back with the poster. On the left-hand side was a big photograph of Éamon de Valera walking down the street with a briefcase under his arm. On the right-hand side, there were some headings with election promises under each.

'Oh, that's perfect!' said Mrs McGee.

'Wait,' said Charlie, looking at the headings.

'Go on, Charlie. Tell us what you're thinkin',' said Maggie.

'The first heading is *TO THE PEOPLE OF IRELAND* and there's a space below it. Why don't we write *ESPECIALLY TO OUR NO. 1 SUPPORTER, THE PIG FARMER*?'

'Good idea, lad,' said a man's voice in the room. A pencil was produced and Charlie wrote the words in big capital letters.

'Next heading is *TO THE YOUNG PEOPLE*. What'll we write in the space under that?' asked Charlie.

'What about *AND THE AULD ONES*?' asked Lilly.

This was duly done.

'All right. Next, we have *TO OUR OPPONENTS.*'

'What does that mean, Ma?' asked one of the McGee girls.

'The people against Fianna Fáil,' she answered.

'I know what to put there,' said Tom. '*STOP CALLING YOUR PIGS AFTER US!*'

There was great laughter at this and Charlie wrote it.

'The last line says *WALK WITH US TOWARDS A NEW IRELAND*,' said Lilly. She leaned over and whispered in my ear. I took up the pencil and drew a silhouette of the Pig Farmer beside it, complete with cap and walking stick. Charlie added a speech bubble coming out of her mouth, with 'I love Fianna Fáil' written in it.

'Here you are, Mrs Hanlon,' I said. 'She's out at the moment. You'll have to hurry to get it done before she comes back.'

'Anyone have a hammer and nail?' asked Mrs Hanlon.

'I have,' said Mrs Perrin.

Minutes later, we all crowded at the door, and the people in the hall stood back to let us watch Mrs Hanlon hammer the poster on the door of the front parlour, where the Pig Farmer lived. Sconsie was sitting on the stairs, balancing a cup of tea on a saucer.

'Toasting the Missus,' he said, holding up the cup. 'God be good to her and grant her a safe passage to his kingdom.'

He stood up when he saw the poster being nailed onto the door. Asking Mr Evans to read it for him as he 'never took to the readin'' himself, he laughed heartily when he heard what was on it. Mrs Hanlon held up the hammer and bowed. This was greeted by clapping and cheering. Teacups and bottles were raised to toast the bravery of the flower seller, who was now squeezing her way through the crowd in our kitchen.

The game went on for another hour. Maggie made sure everyone got sandwiches and a drink. Kate sat close to Patrick. His old teddy tucked under the chair was close enough yet out of sight of the visitors. Charlie and two of his pals were laughing at a story about a newsboy who had saved a swan in the middle of the traffic on City Quay; the boy's name happened to be Billy Swan.

A red hat bobbed among the women blocking the doorway. It was Mona.

'Couldn't leave any earlier,' she called over to Maggie. 'As it was, I left the union meeting before it was over. Here's a bottle for the chisellers.' She held up a bottle of Taylor Keith red lemonade.

'Ah, thanks, Mona,' said Maggie, pushing through to take it.

'What was that on the Pig Farmer's door comin' in?' she asked. Maggie told her about the forfeit and the two sisters giggled at the thought of the Pig Farmer reading it.

Between the laughing and the talking and the neighbours coming in their droves, no one was paying much attention to who was on their way in. But a silence rippled across the room and people started standing aside. For a woman with a walking stick and a slow steady step, the Pig Farmer moved through the crowded kitchen with astonishing speed. Mrs McGee, her back to the door, never saw her come in.

'I'm surprised we haven't heard an explosion yet,' she said. As she spoke the last word, she realised she was the only person in the room talking. She turned around to come face to face with the Pig Farmer. Her white hair, usually in a tight bun, floated over her mealy coloured coat. To have gone out like that, no cap and her hair all over the place, was unheard of. Where on earth had she been, looking like that? One of the little girls from the house next door whimpered.

'Is that the banshee, Ma?'

'Shh,' said her mother. The Pig Farmer ignored this.

'You were saying, Mrs McGee?' she said in the same voice the teachers used in school before they walloped you.

'Oh, it's of no consequence.' Mrs McGee's face was shiny and very red.

Maggie put down the teapot by the fire.

'Can I help you, Mrs Knaggs?'

'You most certainly can by keeping away from my door,' she said, banging her walking stick on the floor. She looked around and pointed it at me. 'It's penance enough to have to share a roof with the likes of them, but to terrorise an old woman in her own home … I'll not stand for it.'

'Now, now, Mrs Knaggs,' said Maggie. 'Don't go blaming Nancy. Remember the poor child's only just lost her mother.'

'That's right,' said Barney Hogan. 'Sure, you know yourself, it's only a bit of harmless fun to put in the night.'

'Harmless fun?' said the Pig Farmer. 'All I can say is it doesn't surprise me how low you'd stoop for your so-called *harmless fun*.'

Charlie was going to say something but Lilly put her hand on his arm to stop him. The lively chat and laughter of a few moments earlier had disappeared like smoke up the chimney. Granny's clock – what she always referred to as a Murphy heirloom – tick-tocked on the mantelpiece. The Pig Farmer smirked, and the sight of her inside our kitchen and Ma laid out made me speak up.

'If you aren't here to pay respects to my mother, I'd prefer if you left.'

'I'd be lyin' if I said I was here to do that. But I'll leave you with this warning: if any of you are brazen enough ever to deface my door again, so help me God, you'll live to regret it.' She took her time moving towards the door and spoke out of the corner of her mouth.

'The one that's talking about respect! The living deserves respect the same as the dead. Hah! What would you expect … given where the lot of them came from?'

The women crowding the doorway stood back and let her

through. Nobody spoke. It was like the evil queen from Snow White had come among us and left a trail of gloom after her. Tom found his voice first.

'What did she say about where we came from?'

'Don't know what she was saying,' said Mrs McGee. 'Anyway, isn't she always spoiling for a fight?'

'The state of her with her hair down! What was she thinking of going out like that?' said Maggie. 'I vote we forget about her. Let's get a song going to keep the spirits up. Mona, will you get us started? Sing us one of the songs from work.'

In the Phoenix Laundry, the women often sang songs as they washed and dried the clothes. But it wasn't only on account of where she worked that Mona was asked to sing. Everyone loved her sweet voice. She smiled and patted me on the arm.

'Never mind that Pig Farmer, love. You know as well as I do that when God was handing out hearts, she was hidin' behind the door. And speakin' of hearts—' She closed her eyes and started singing 'The Rose of San Antone'.

Mona's rich voice filled the room. Everyone joined in the chorus. Maggie was right. The singing *did* lift our spirits. We could even hear Sconsie in full voice out on the stairs.

Chapter Six

The day after the funeral, I slid Aunt Gretta's telegram in behind the clock. It had two sentences to say that she couldn't make the long journey on account of her bad hip and that she insisted on paying for the funeral. I was relieved. Everything was so dear now; the collection hadn't covered all the money we owed.

I went back to school on Monday.

'Sorry about your mother,' said Mrs McCullagh to me in the yard before we went in. She was our teacher in Sixth Class. I was taken aback. These were the first kind words she ever spoke to me. She was a culchie, like all the teachers, and had taught me in First Class when we arrived from Leeds. I remember feeling mortified when she used to make fun of my accent. By the time I was in Sixth, my English accent was gone, but she criticised me constantly; if it wasn't spellings in my English essays, it was the fact that my hair was in my eyes. If it wasn't my hair, it was the blobs of ink on my writing copy.

I saw most of the girls during the three days of the wake. But when I went back to school, I was surprised that, except for Lilly, not one person mentioned that my mother had died. 'Mother dead, funeral over, back to school, now get on with it,' seemed to be the way. Even Jacinta O'Shea, whose mother had died only a year before, hardly looked at me. That made me think about how I had behaved when *her* mother died. I never said anything to her either. One kind word to her could have made all the difference – and here was I longing for the same.

As for Aunt Gretta, true to her word, a letter and a postal order arrived the following Wednesday and I went straight to Marlborough Street and settled the bill with Mr Farrell, the undertaker.

Inside the envelope, I discovered something else: a photo of Ma and Da when they were courting. There was Da's big handsome face looking at the camera as if he was amused by some story he had just heard.

By staring at the photo, I hoped that some memories of him might come back. I had so few. But that wasn't surprising. When we lived in Leeds and he was working in Tetley's Brewery, he was hardly ever home. His ma, Nanny Kidd, lived in a flat in town. On his days off, she called on Da constantly to come over to fix things and lift things. When the war broke out, he joined the army and we came to Ireland. I never saw him after that.

In the picture, Ma was smiling, her head resting on Da's shoulder. She looked about sixteen. People said I had her sallow skin and long face, but staring at the photo, all I could see was Kate. I was surprised Aunt Gretta had sent this picture; she never had much time for Da and was against the pair of them marrying so young. Ma told me about the rows she had with Aunt Gretta when she told her she was going to be married. At one point, she thought they'd never speak again. I turned the photo around to see if the date was written on the back, and in capital letters it said: FROM YOUR NANNY IN LEEDS. So that explained it: Aunt Gretta was only passing it on.

'What does Aunt Gretta say?' asked Kate, looking up from her book. Tom was washing potatoes in the basin on the table. He dried his hands and took up the photo I had put down.

'She says she's been to see Nanny in Leeds to tell her about Ma,' I said. 'Nanny gave her the photo to send to us. Aunt Gretta said Nanny's too poorly to write to us, but to pass on her sympathy.'

'Hmm. "Too poorly" – Ma would have some comment to make about that,' said Kate.

'More like "couldn't be bothered",' said Tom. 'Any other news?'

'Hardly anything else. It was a funny kind of letter. Probably upset about Ma and couldn't think straight.'

'What do you mean "funny"?' asked Kate.

'The way it was written – not very friendly. There was none of the usual fuss about arrangements to come over.'

'Do we still have to wait until school is over to move?' asked Tom.

'We have to wait a bit longer,' I said. 'She said she has to get the place ready for us. It'll be a while before she can send for us.'

'A while?' said Kate. I could hear the disappointment in her voice.

'She's slowed down with her sore hip. It takes longer to do things,' I suggested.

'At least we won't have to go back to the red-brick slaughterhouse in September,' said Tom, using the nickname we all had for the school. 'I can't wait to get away from the Master and his Irish grammar.'

'Funny enough, I'll miss Irish,' said Kate. 'Mrs Tierney says it's my best subject.'

'Every subject is your best subject, Brainy Box,' said Tom.

'Will I still have to do multiplication tables?' asked Patrick.

'Yes, you will. I know you don't like them but everyone has to learn them,' said Kate.

'As we're not going for a while, we've got to think about the rent,' I said. 'I'm going to have to leave school and get a job. It'll have to be full-time.'

'I could get a Saturday job like some of the girls in my class,' said Kate.

'And I was thinking I could start selling the papers,' said Tom.

'That's a great idea, isn't it, Nancy?' asked Kate. She watched me closely, the way she used to watch Ma when she was trying to persuade her to do something.

'Ma wouldn't have been in favour, but we have to do what we can for ourselves now. Let me talk to Charlie,' I said. 'He'd be a great help to get you started.'

'*Herald* or *Mail*!' shouted Tom like the newsboys on the street.

'God, isn't he a natural?' said Kate, laughing.

'Is that Tom I hear sellin' the readers?' shouted a voice outside. I put my head out the window. Mrs McGee was looking out of her window above us. 'I'm lookin' for a *Herald*, Nancy.'

'He was only having a go at the call, Mrs McGee,' I said back up to her. 'But I'm sure he wouldn't mind runnin' out and gettin' one for you.'

Tom made a face but left directly.

★ ★ ★

On Thursday evening, Kate and I went through Ma's clothes. I kept her two best skirts and one of her dresses. Kate insisted on keeping a lace collar Granny had owned and had given to Ma.

When I came across the soft green cardigan that she had knitted during the winter, I bundled it into the bag quickly. Ma had been planning to wear it in Leeds once we returned. Kate and I had both cried enough this morning. My eyes were smarting and my throat felt sore. I tied the bundle of clothes up in a big cotton shawl and left it on the kitchen table.

Mona called in on her way home from work. She said her friend would get a good price for this lot at the Daisy Market.

'Grand big bundle,' said Mona. Her fair hair was tucked under a crocheted beret. Her lips, usually dark red, were pale, but her cheeks had large red blotches on them.

'So good to sit down,' she said.

'Were you runnin'?' asked Patrick.

'No, unless you're asking me was I runnin' a machine in the laundry. I was on the hydros today.'

'Hydros?' asked Patrick.

'Big machines for drying,' said Mona. 'I had to drag the clothes out of the washing machines and put them into the hydros to dry them.'

'That doesn't sound too hard,' said Patrick.

'It does when you have to lift heavy wet clothes that are steamin' hot from the washing machines,' said Mona.

'Did you find anything in the pockets this week?' Patrick loved Mona's stories.

'Funny you should ask that,' said Mona with a little smile at the corner of her lips. 'When I was working in the Check-In Room earlier in the week, a glass eyeball rolled out of a trousers pocket. The trouble was I couldn't figure out which trousers.'

'And what did you do?' asked Patrick, his own eyes wide.

'I went up to my boss and I showed her the eye. "Oh, I know who owns that," says she. "It's Mr Carr from Iona Road."

'"How do you know?" says I.

'"Sure, don't I see him every morning at the bus stop? When the double-decker bus comes, he pops his eye out and throws it up high and catches it."'

'Why does he do that?' asked Patrick.

'To see if there's any room upstairs on the bus!' said Mona, which made us all laugh.

Mona buried her face in the cool cotton shawl that covered the bundle on the table.

'Ooh, so cool.' We could just make out the muffled words. After a moment, she lifted her face, winked at Patrick and scooped up the bundle.

'Right, I'll pass these on to Della. She'll see you right. I'll be callin' into her tomorrow on the way to the union meeting.'

'What's the latest?' I asked. 'Will yiz be going on strike?'

'We might be. Up to a few weeks ago, I'd still be at work now. Imagine – after a full day of standing on your feet – not being able to leave until nine o'clock! But the union's told all the bosses that we're not doin' any more overtime until we get two weeks' paid holidays.'

'Paid for doing nothing for two weeks?' said Kate. She was only saying what we were all thinking. Two weeks seemed like a long time to be off.

'To make up for killin' ourselves the other fifty,' said Mona. 'You'd want to see the conditions we work in, Kate. Dreadful! That's why it's great to have the union – someone to protect us and fight for us. If refusin' to do overtime doesn't work, you can be sure we *will* be goin' on strike.'

'What'll happen to all the dirty clothes?' asked Patrick.

'Hmmm. The dirty clothes will have to wash themselves,' said Mona.

'Like this?' Patrick grabbed his gansey in two places and started rubbing them frantically against each other. Mona threw her head back and laughed one of her laughs that always got everybody joining in. She patted the bundle of clothes.

'I'm headin' off. I'll see you at second Mass on Sunday.'

Kate and I always met up with Lilly and Mona at eleven o'clock Mass in the Tin Church in Sean MacDermott Street.

★ ★ ★

On Friday evening, the smell of fried fish from the dinner still lingered in our kitchen. I lifted a pot half-filled with water onto the fire. I needed more to wash the dirty dishes and Tom took off with a bucket to fill at the tap outside.

'Can't wait to move to Aunt Gretta's house. No more lugging buckets of water in from an outside tap,' he said, banging the enamel bucket onto the table when he got back.

'No more having to scare the rats away to get to the toilet in the yard,' said Kate, emptying the bucket into the pot on the fire.

'No more bugs to go after and no more mice!' I said. 'And we won't have to smell the bugs either.'

'There could be mice in Aunt Gretta's,' said Patrick.

'But it's easier to get rid of them in a new house,' I said.

I dipped my finger into the water to check if it was warm enough.

'I'm lookin' forward to having running water indoors and a machine to wash clothes,' I said.

'When do you think Aunt Gretta will let us know when we can come over?' asked Tom.

'Oh, I'd say she'll let us know soon enough.' Something made me cross my fingers for good luck as I said this. Maybe the changes to her house would be finished quicker than Aunt Gretta thought and we would be on our way to Leeds sooner rather than later. But in the meantime, us Kidds were in Summerhill and we had to make the best of it.

Chapter Seven

I sat down for a few minutes in Ma's chair and fell asleep. Two crisp knocks on the door woke me up.

'Rent!' said a voice outside. It was Mr Williams, the rent collector. We always called him 'the frontman'.

I scrambled over to the dresser for the money. I had counted it out this morning, so it was only a matter of grabbing it from the shelf. I took the rent book out of the biscuit tin.

'Sorry about your mother,' mumbled the frontman. The big, blocky former guard looked down at his black boots, then glanced quickly around to see if anyone was listening in. He squinted his eyes and added: 'Still able to pay the rent?'

'Yes, Mr Williams,' I said, handing him the rent book first and then the money. He counted out my coins.

'Short sixpence,' he said. He held a big leathery hand out with the coins I had given him, before he dropped them into his cloth bag.

I stared at the coins. I definitely had the right amount ready.

'Wait a minute,' I said. The Pig Farmer was playing her favourite hymn on her gramophone.

Bring flowers of the rarest, bring blossoms the fairest.

The frontman hummed along as he waited. I ran back to the dresser inside. All the coins were gone from where I had left them. I'd have to go into the shopping money. Then I realised that Kate had taken all of it before setting off to go to Price's to get the meat and afterwards to Moran's for the milk.

'Hurry up, will you?' came an impatient voice at the door.

'What's the problem, Mr Williams?' came another voice. It was Mrs McGee's. I came out to the hall.

'Kate must have taken some of the rent money to do the shoppin',' I said to her. 'I'm short sixpence.'

'Wait here,' said Mrs McGee, and she disappeared up the stairs to her own place.

'I could do without this delay,' said Mr Williams, checking his watch. Mrs McGee came running down the stairs.

'Here's thruppence. Surely the other few pennies could wait until next week? With the mother hardly cold in the grave?'

'Full rent to be collected. Them's the rules,' said the frontman, dropping the extra money into the bag.

'Have you no heart?' shouted Mrs McGee. 'The poor girl's lost her mother and is trying her best to look after her family!'

'And *I'm* trying to keep my job,' he said calmly.

Mrs Perrin called down from the landing: 'How much are you short, love?'

'Threepence.'

She came down the stairs, plunged her hand into the pocket of her apron and held out three pennies to the frontman.

'There's your money,' she said. The two women stood each side of the frontman, their hands on their hips.

'I think I'll hold on to this rent book,' said Mr Williams after marking it. 'You seem very young to be in charge of it.'

'Oh, for God's sake, will you leave that with the girl?' said Mrs McGee. 'Don't you know the cloth she's cut from? She'll mind it the way her ma and her granny did before her.'

'Hmmph!' said the frontman, handing the book back to me.

'And tell that fella in that no-good Corpo we *still* need another tap in the yard,' she called after him as he climbed the stairs. Our landlord was a member of Dublin Corporation, as many a Dublin landlord was.

'Yes, yes,' he said, moving faster. He panted his way up to the next landing. 'He's looking for the right man to do the job.'

'It's only a pipe and tap we need; we're not lookin' for bleedin' Niagara Falls,' called out Mrs McGee, and the two women laughed.

'I'll pay you both back,' I said. 'And thanks.'

'You're all right, love, whenever you have it,' said Mrs McGee. She went to the bottom of the stairs. 'We're on our way up, Mr Williams. Don't worry; you'll get your money.'

Instead of going back inside, I decided to track Patrick down. I had a feeling he might know where the missing money was.

He'd been in the kitchen before I fell asleep. More than likely he was playing with Brendan in the Diamond. I tore up the path and turned into the archway at the top of the twenty-seven steps. Somebody behind me had started to whistle 'Nancy (with the Laughing Face)'. I knew that whistle. It was Charlie.

'Hi,' he said cheerfully when I turned around. 'How are you getting on, Nancy?'

'Managing. But now that you ask, I could do with a favour.'

'I'm all ears.'

'We're thinking of getting Tom into sellin' the papers.'

'And you want me to help?' asked Charlie.

'If you could, it'd be great.'

He took my hand.

'Of course.' I looked around to see if anyone was watching. Two boys were jumping up and down the last few steps. Charlie squeezed my hand, his cap sideways as he grinned at me. We were always joking with him that he was a great whistler because of that gap between his teeth. His face came very close to mine.

'Ah, look at the pair of them kissin',' shouted one of the boys at the bottom of the steps. But Charlie had dropped our hands and our lips never met. He looked down at the boys and shook his fist at them.

'Tell Tom I'll call around for him tomorrow,' he said. 'He can come and do the morning round with me to see what it's like. Saturday's a good day to do it. Will he be able to get up at half-past five?'

'He will.' I ran down two more steps and called back, 'Thanks, Charlie.'

I continued down the steps. Patrick and Brendan liked to play around the air-raid shelter. I spotted them standing with their backs to me, counting out something in their hands.

'Patrick Kidd!' I shouted.

He jumped and turned around. I came closer to them.

'Did you take sixpence out of the rent money?'

'No,' said Patrick, turning several shades of red.

'You're lyin' and I know it,' I whispered into his ear. I grabbed his hand and opened it.

'Where did you get that money?'

'All right,' he said crossly. 'I did take it. But for a good reason.'

'Yes?'

'I'm goin' to buy a dog.'

'What?'

'Mickser Doyle said his dog had five pups and I could have one of them for sixpence.'

'Mickser doesn't live with us. You have to ask *me* about dogs first.'

'Mam said I could have a dog when we move back to Leeds.' His bottom lip was turning down, but I couldn't let that change my mind.

'We're still in Dublin. What were you thinkin'?'

'I was thinkin' that he could get used to us and move over with us. And wouldn't he be good to chase the rats in the yard while we're still in Summerhill?'

'We don't have enough money for a dog, Patrick. Not at the moment. Look, I'm taking this money back off you and you have to promise not to go near it again.'

His eyes started to fill with tears.

'I was looking forward to bringin' him home.'

'Sorry, Patrick. We can't have a dog now. Why don't yourself and Brendan come home with me and I'll make you a nice cup of cocoa?'

'What about Mickser? He's waiting for me to come over.'

'Mickser? Shame on him for trying to squeeze money out of our family. Let him wait. It won't do him a bit of harm.'

* * *

Tom came back on Saturday afternoon with sore feet, an empty stomach, but a happy heart. Charlie had told him he was a natural when it came to selling 'the readers' and that he could start a proper round on Wednesday if he wanted to take it on.

'Will you have to wear a cap like Charlie?' asked Patrick. He loved Charlie who joked and played with him and made him feel like 'one of the boys'. The thought of his big brother going to work with Charlie put Tom into a higher group of human beings.

'Don't have to, but I'd like to get one,' said Tom.

'We'll have some money from Ma's clothes tomorrow,' I said. 'Might be able to get you sorted then.'

On my way towards the Tin Church the following morning, I felt my sleeve being pulled.

'Made a nice bit of money, those clothes,' said Mona. She wore a navy jacket that showed off her narrow little waist. Like Lilly, she had a high forehead. She pressed the money into my hand. I had a quick look at the amount before slipping it into the pocket of my jacket.

'Thanks, Mona.'

I was about to ask her if her friend found it easy to sell them when a shrill wolf whistle came from behind us. I blushed and half expected to see Charlie when I looked back. But there was no sign of Charlie – only Jemmy and Mickser.

'For God's sake, will you have a bit of respect going into the chapel?' said Mona.

'It wasn't me!' Jemmy protested, holding up his hands.

'I wouldn't waste my breath whistling at the likes of you,' said Mickser, a sour look on his face.

Mona made a face at him and we blessed ourselves with holy water from the font on the way in. We sat into a pew on the women's side a little more than halfway up the church. Women scurried into seats around us to be sitting down before the priest came out. The Pig Farmer hobbled up the aisle towards her usual perch in the front seat. She had just passed us when a little girl stepped out of a seat in front of her, almost tripping her up. The old woman managed to stop herself from falling, but dropped her missal; the prayer book with its scuffed black leather cover fell out of her grasp and onto the floor, a dozen or so holy pictures cascading out of it.

If the mother of the little girl did not have a longstanding grievance with the Pig Farmer over the smell of the pigs in the yard, she might have picked the missal up. Instead, she pulled her little daughter back into the seat and, tight-lipped, looked ahead as if nothing had happened. The Pig Farmer tried to bend down and hold onto the walking stick at the same time, but when the stick wobbled, she gave up.

Nobody came forward to pick the missal up. The Pig Farmer looked around to see if there was someone she could ask. Kate, sitting on the outside of the pew and watching what was happening, jumped up and stepped out into the aisle. She knelt and gathered all the holy pictures into one neat bundle. One caught her eye, and she paused for a few seconds before slipping it in with the others. The missal was duly plucked from the floor and, stuffed with the pictures between its pages, handed to the old woman who stared at Kate with her mouth open. She glanced over at us as if to check was this really one of the Kidds helping her? With the black missal firmly in her gloved hand, she leaned slightly forward.

'Thank you,' she whispered and took off again towards the front pew.

'Goody-Two-Shoes,' said Lilly under her breath as Kate sat back on the seat.

'I can't believe you helped that heartless old biddy,' I whispered.

'Just because *she's* heartless, doesn't mean *I* have to be.'

'What did you see that time?'

'Her husband's memorial card.'

'Martin Knaggs? What did he look like?'

'Handsome. He was wearing his army uniform.'

The bell rang. Fr Comiskey arrived out onto the altar in his white vestments, his deep voice filling the church with the Latin prayers. He had a talent for preaching and his sermons were popular with young and old, so once communion was over and the coins dropped into the collection boxes that had been passed around, we eased our way onto our seats looking forward to what he had to say. He removed his outer vestment, padded across to the pulpit, climbed the steps into it and was getting ready to speak when he was stopped by the piercing sound of the same wolf whistle that we had heard on the way in. Kate, Lilly, Mona and I looked at each other, puzzled. A titter rippled across the church. Fr Comiskey's face darkened.

'What has the world come to when somebody sees fit to be doing the likes of that in the House of God?' He looked around to see if he could pick out the offender. The laughter had stopped and the church was eerily silent. He paused, checking to see if we were all ready to listen before he started again.

'Today I'm going to—'

'Sit down and have a cup of tea,' shouted a voice.

At that moment, a green-and-yellow parrot flew from the back of the church towards the statue of St Anthony in the top corner, perching on the bald part of St Anthony's head. This was greeted by some stifled laughter.

'And no swearing!' said the parrot, and he coughed like an old man.

By now nobody was holding back and laughter filled the church.

Fr Comiskey clasped the pulpit, shook his head and grinned.

'I was going to talk about foul language, but our little feathered friend got in ahead of me.' This brought on another wave of laughter. The parrot started to sing:

In Dublin's fair city, where the girls are so pretty…

The place erupted again.

'Given the colours he's wearing, I think the "Rose of Tralee" would be a more fitting song to sing.' As Fr Comiskey was a Kerryman, this went down well. Then the parrot wolf-whistled again and started singing in another language:

La donna è mobile …

'That's opera,' whispered Kate into my ear when she'd managed to stop laughing.

'I think we'll have to—' began Fr Comiskey.

'Sit down and have a cup of tea,' shouted the parrot again.

Fr Comiskey held his hands up in surrender.

'*La donna è mobile*,' sang the parrot.

'Could the men in charge of the collection boxes close the windows, please?' the priest said. 'That way we'll be able to catch our little intruder and return him to his owner.'

A man climbed the steps of the pulpit and whispered something into Fr Comiskey's ear.

'I have been reliably informed that we are in the presence of one Caruso McCabe who belongs to Molly McCabe of Rutland Street. Could somebody go down and ask her to collect her little companion, please?'

There was more laughter at this.

'The archbishop won't be impressed when he hears a parrot upstaged me at Mass, but in the circumstances, I think it's best to postpone my sermon 'til next Sunday,' said Fr Comiskey, stepping down from the pulpit.

Caruso in the meantime was making a grand tour of the statues of the church. He left St Anthony and flew a couple of yards over to St Patrick, balancing nicely on the top of his crozier, from where the parrot's beady eyes had a good look at his audience. St Joseph, standing at the far side of the altar, was his next target. This time the parrot decided to take the scenic route and swooped over the heads of the first few rows of Mass-goers.

'Wouldn't it be gas if he did his business on top of the Pig Farmer's cap?' whispered Lilly. I couldn't help giggling. The Pig Farmer sat as still as any of the statues in the church. I could imagine her saying, like Queen Victoria, 'We are not amused.'

The parrot, on the other hand, was hugely enjoying himself. From his perch on the lily in St Joseph's hand, he called, 'Sit down and have a cup of tea' several times before flying over to the statue of the Sacred Heart. After one last *La donna è mobile,* the parrot quietened down.

By the time we were singing the final hymn, Molly McCabe had arrived with her birdcage and, with hardly any coaxing, Caruso left the Sacred Heart for the comfort of his little home.

Everybody exited the Tin Church with smiles on their faces – or almost everybody. Mona turned around when she felt a tap on her shoulder.

'Told you it wasn't me,' Jemmy growled with a toss of his head as he crossed to the far side of the street.

Chapter Eight

Thanks to the money from Ma's clothes, Tom left the house at half-past five on Wednesday morning, a new cap on his head and money in his pocket to buy the papers he was going to sell. Newsboys called this their 'stork' money. Charlie had arranged to meet him at the *Herald* office in Prince's Street and the two of them took off along Abbey Street. I warned Tom to keep an eye on the time. He was still at school and had to make it back in time for the Morning Offering in Mr O'Sullivan's class. If he was late, it meant getting six sharp slaps with a cane on each hand.

Kate and I were only in the door that afternoon when Tom ran in, threw his school bag in the corner and fell into Ma's chair.

'Well, Tom, how did it go?' I asked, but before I got to the word 'go', Tom's eyes were closing. He put his hand into his pocket and pulled out all the change he had made selling the papers. Kate pounced on it. Six shillings and sixpence! Kate let it fall with a lovely jingle into Ma's money bowl on the dresser.

'So tired....' Tom muttered. 'Trying to stay awake in school ... geography lesson ... all about India.' His head dropped and he was fast asleep. His cap fell off onto the floor. Kate picked it up and put it on, pushing her two plaits underneath.

'I could pass as a newsboy, couldn't I?' said Kate, looking at herself in the small mirror on the wall near the window.

'No, you could not,' I said, grabbing the cap.

'Wouldn't it be work, though, Nancy?'

'It would, but we've enough on our plate with Tom working without a badge. To have you out there on the streets with the boys – even if you were only pretending to be one – I couldn't think of it, Kate.'

'Could you not, Sis?' said Kate. 'Hmm, whatever I get, if I manage to get a job at all, I won't make anything like Tom.'

'True, but don't forget every penny counts.' I checked to make sure that the table was clean before I put Tom's cap on the oilcloth with the red and yellow flowers that Granny bought when we came back from Leeds. Granny wasn't on my mind now, but I knew who was: Charlie's handsome face beneath *his* newsboy cap.

Kate had bought a pig's head from the butcher at a good price and it was almost cooked. As I lifted the pot off the fire, a knock came to the door. It was Mrs Hanlon from the basement, standing with a can in her hand.

'Got the smell of the bacon. Wonder if you can spare the water off it?' she asked, holding the can out. 'It'd be lovely for the spuds and cabbage.'

'Come on in,' I said. She took a few steps into the kitchen. Tom was still fast asleep in Ma's chair.

'He started work today,' I said. 'Selling the papers.'

'Work?' she said, looking at Tom. 'I thought yiz were all headin' over to your aunt in England.'

'We are, but not for a while,' I said. 'She's to get the place ready for us.'

I took the can and placed it on the table. The room filled with the smell of the bacon as I tipped all of the greasy water into the can. This was probably the nearest thing to meat her family would get this week.

'Sure, he'll help bring in a few bob,' she said, nodding over at Tom.

'And all going well, we'll be doing the same,' I said. 'I'm leavin' school as soon as I can get a job.'

'And I'm looking for Saturday work,' said Kate.

'They're lookin' for a cleaner in Babywear if you're interested,' said Mrs Hanlon, carefully holding the can by its handle. 'A few hours' work on a Saturday morning.'

'That place in Mary Street?'

'The very one. I could put a word in for you,' said Mrs Hanlon as Kate held the door for her.

'If you could, that'd help,' said Kate.

'Leave it with me,' she said.

The front door must have been open as our door closed with a bang. Tom shot up.

'The capital of India is New Delhi,' he said.

'Silly! You're not in school now,' said Kate. 'Come on, dinner's almost ready.'

Tom stretched his arms out.

'Didn't I make a nice bit of money?' he said.

'You did,' said Kate.

'Charlie was a great help, showing me all the good pitches. But he warned me that the money wouldn't always be as good as today. He makes up for the slow days by going out at night when the pubs are closing, to sell early editions. Said there's good money to be made at that time.'

'He's older than you, don't forget,' I said. 'You'll not be out at that hour. Where did you go today?'

'Mainly Moore Street and Parnell Street,' he said. 'And who do you think was over in Moore Street haggling with the dealers?'

'Maggie?' I suggested.

'Far cry from Maggie. The Pig Farmer! If that wasn't enough, I had the bad luck to bump into her again later on when I was on my own. I finished over at the Pro-Cathedral and there she was, strolling down Marlborough Street, talking the ear off some auld fella. He'd a long navy coat on and a face like a skull, he was that thin.'

'Was he wearing glasses?' asked Kate.

'He was. Do you know him?'

'Don't know his name, but I've seen the Pig Farmer talking to him before.'

'When she spotted me, she gave him a dig in the ribs and pointed to me. I passed by and ignored the pair of them, but I knew she was talking about me.'

'Wonder what she was natterin' about,' I said. 'Did you tell Charlie about it after?'

'I did. He said not to mind the Pig Farmer. Let her point her old 'crubeen' if she wants to.'

* * *

Come half-past eight the next morning, I was leaning against the red-brick wall of the school, waiting for Miss Dalton, the principal. It was raining, and she moved up the footpath beneath a large black umbrella. She was startled when she saw me at the door.

'Merciful hour,' she said, closing her umbrella and shaking the rain off it. 'Will you come in out of the rain, Nancy Kidd?' She unlocked the door of the school and ushered me in.

'How are you getting on?' she said in a softer voice. 'Of course, it's still early days.'

'It is, but we still have the bills to pay,' I said. We stood in the dark corridor as she untied a scarf that was around her head. 'With Ma gone and all, I need to work, Miss.'

'Need to work? Is there nobody to look after you?'

'We're going back to Leeds – to Ma's Aunt Gretta – but

that's not happening until later in the summer. I'll need more than Da's pension to keep us going while we're here.'

She took off her glasses and wiped them with a hankie.

'Have you started looking yet?'

'No, Miss, but I heard there could be temporary jobs going in some of the clothes factories.'

'And you'll need a reference. Let me talk to Mrs McCullagh.'

My heart sank when I heard this. Even though my sewing was the one thing Mrs McCullagh couldn't find fault with, she could never bring herself to say that it was good. What sort of reference would she give me?

As if Miss Dalton was reading my mind, she asked what teacher I'd had last year.

'Mrs Tierney,' I answered. 'She taught Ma as well, Miss.'

'Right. Leave it with me, Nancy,' she said. 'And don't go back outside. Sit down on the bench there until the bell rings.'

★ ★ ★

On Friday afternoon, a girl from Third Class came to our classroom and announced that the principal wanted to see me. I quietly opened the door into Miss Dalton's classroom; all the girls were busy writing. She beckoned me towards her table, and pressed a white envelope into my hand, together with a sheet of paper torn out of a copy.

'When Mrs Tierney heard you were looking for a job, she gave me this,' she whispered. The page had a name and address written on it. 'Someone she knows works there.'

'Thanks, Miss.' I read the address: Mandel's Clothing Factory, Foley Street.

'The woman's name is Miss Curran. They've openings for runners – for temporary jobs. Mrs Tierney told her that you're a good diligent worker. Don't let her down, Nancy.'

I thanked her again and slipped back to my own classroom. I was dying to tell Lilly, but she hadn't been at school the last couple of days – probably minding the twins. It felt very strange for me to be starting a job – my very first job – and for Lilly not to know.

Later, Kate and I headed up Rutland Street towards Summerhill, past a cluster of girls from school. They were talking about a film called *The Song of Bernadette*. You could stand and talk about films when you had mothers at home to look after you, I thought wistfully. I went through the list of messages to buy on the way home. Mrs Gaynor's fish stall at the archway was my first stop.

'Get the last of the Howth herrings!' I could hear her call once I turned the corner into Summerhill.

Kate was going over to Mary Street to ask about the cleaning job. Our days of dawdling on the steps, chatting at the street corners, playing games and telling stories were well and truly over.

★ ★ ★

Kate started as a cleaner at nine o'clock on Saturday morning, thanks to Mrs Hanlon's word with one of the regular cleaners. The pay wasn't great, but as Kate said herself, it was still a plus in our money instead of a minus. Tom was out selling the papers. *They* were both working, but the house still needed looking after. I sent Patrick down to Reilly's to get a few messages. Once he was gone, I grabbed the bucket and headed down to the tap in the yard to fill it for washing the clothes. Some of it spilt on the way back through the kitchen. I poured what was left into the pot that hung over the fire and headed out through the hall with the bucket. Sconsie was sitting on the third step.

'If you give me some fancy bread, I'll bring the water up for you,' he said, standing up. I stopped and was about to tell him I was managing grand when the foolishness of that struck me. Of course, I should say 'yes' and make my life easier.

'Done, Sconsie,' I said. 'I'll even throw in a cup of tea with it.'

I gave him the bucket. Back inside, I took out the tin tub, the washboard and the carbolic soap. It wasn't raining; I wouldn't have to set up a line inside. By the time Patrick came back, Sconsie was sitting on the step with an enamel mug of tea and some fancy bread and I was hanging the clothes on the line out the back window. The palliasses we slept on needed to be stuffed with fresh straw. Ma hated this job and now I knew why. It added so much to the work to be done. *They can wait another week,* I said to myself as I dragged them off the floor and piled them onto Ma's bed. Once the floor was clear, I handed the broom to Patrick to do the sweeping. I made a mental note about buying some DDT to kill the bugs. The walls were worse than usual.

'That blessed horsehair,' Ma used to say. 'If the walls weren't so full of it, we mightn't have as many creepy crawlies.'

When the clothes were done, I used the water in the tub to scrub the floors. As I moved a chair away from the table to wash underneath, a mouse appeared. Once he saw me, he darted across the floor into Ma's bedroom. Earlier in the week, I had got Tom to check under Ma's bed and he reported that there was a hole in the skirting board in the corner. I took note in my head to get something to block the hole and buy a few new traps.

Kate was coming in the door as I was leaving to go to the shops.

'God, I worked for this,' she said, jingling some coins in her hand. She popped them into the money bowl and fell into Ma's old chair. 'This chair was all I could think of on the way home. I thought I'd finish that Enid Blyton book from the library, but I can't keep my eyes open…'

As she sank further into the chair, her eyes closed. She

hadn't even taken off her coat. I'd planned on going over to Lilly's later on to tell her about my job. But after washing the clothes, hanging them out, cleaning the place, shopping, cooking dinner and sorting the clothes and ironing some of them, I couldn't convince my two feet to bring me down the steps to the Diamond. Anyway, I'd see her at second Mass on Sunday.

But Sunday came and neither Lilly nor Mona appeared at the chapel. I planned to pop over to Weavers' later, but dinner had to be cooked and two more mice had to be dealt with. We borrowed Mrs Perrin's cat – a big orange tom called Ginger – and gave him the run of the place for the afternoon. He managed to catch one. By the time he was returned to his owner, my legs were aching. I was in bed by nine o'clock and, other than Sconsie singing 'Kevin Barry' out in the hall, I heard nothing until the next morning. I'd have to see Lilly some evening during the week.

Chapter Nine

Come Monday, when the church bell chimed half-past eight, I was standing in the lobby of Mandel's Clothing Factory, staring through the huge window into the workroom. Rows of women crouched close to the needles of their sewing machines, which were going so fast, I felt as if I was watching one of the funny bits in the films where they make everything speed up. Behind them, men and women stood at counters, cutting material. Through thick clouds of steam, I could see some men pressing trousers and jackets with big irons attached to long cords from the ceiling. The place smelled of heated wool and machine-oil. A girl passed by the window with some straight pins sticking out of her mouth. She nodded when she saw me and I remembered her being in Sixth Class two years ago, but I couldn't remember her name.

A tall man in a tweed suit was talking to another man – one of the cutters. He looked up and saw me. He continued talking for a few minutes before walking through the aisle between the machinists and making his way towards the lobby. I could see now that he was wearing a black apron over his suit. He opened the door. The machines all sounded much louder. He closed it behind him and spoke to me.

'Miss Kidd?' he asked.

'Yes, sir,' I answered.

'Just in time,' he said, looking at his watch. His eyes moved from my face down to my shoes. Next, he grabbed both my hands and examined them.

'Good. Clean hands,' he said. 'I'm Mr Niblock. The workroom's this way. Follow me.'

He had an English accent and his voice made me think of Jim Lightfoot, our next-door-neighbour in Leeds. He led me into the workroom, through the drone of sewing machines. Nobody smiled or said 'hello', and the last girl I passed could have been tasting sour milk with the face on her.

'You'll be expected to bring garments to different people in the workroom, to go to our sister company over beside the Ha'penny Bridge, when required, and to go to shops and the post office. You will also be asked to do some work in the workroom, as Miss Curran will explain.'

'Good morning, Miss Kidd.' A small woman with red curly hair cut short came forward and herded me to a table where a boy's jacket was laid out. It had big white basting stitches in it still. A small white tool lay beside it.

'For the moment you will be working mostly in the workroom. See the jacket here on the table? You're to remove the bastings from the jackets once they're passed to you. There's the bodkin for doing it.' As she spoke, she lifted the smooth white tool with a pointy end. Then she whipped out the stitches at lightning speed. 'Remember you're here on a two-week trial – the same as Miss Popper there at the table in front of you.'

A girl with sallow skin, dark brown eyes and shoulder-length black hair with a fashionable wave in it looked back at me and smiled. She was wearing red lipstick. She looked about eighteen.

'Once you've got the stitches out, bring the jacket over to Miss King.' She bent over and spoke into my ear. 'Mrs Tierney told me about you. Do your best now, girl, and you'll be kept for the summer.'

I smiled at her and was half afraid to talk. All that could be heard was the loud whirr of the sewing machines.

I eased my way into the rhythm of using the bodkin. Snip, snip went the stitches that had been holding the pieces of fabric together before they were machine-stitched. I was up every few minutes to put a jacket at Miss King's table. At half-past ten, all the workers around me stood up and walked out. It was time for our break. Miss Curran brought me out to the kitchen and explained how each person was expected to contribute some tea and sugar for a cuppa at each of the two breaks.

'Joan King is in charge of all that. You saw her inside. Make sure you bring some tomorrow. We've our proper break at one o'clock. Did you bring anything with you?'

'I brought some bread and a bottle of milk,' I told her.

'That'll do you then,' she said.

The men and women moved quickly into the kitchen.

'Every minute of break is precious,' said Miss Curran, whooshing me ahead of her.

A big kettle of water was boiling on the gas cooker beside the biggest teapot I had ever laid eyes on. A dozen mugs with spoons in them stood in the middle of the table. Everything was spotless.

'My turn today,' said one of the women, taking out the tea caddy.

'Did the new girls bring tea with them?' asked one of the men.

'No,' came from the dark-haired girl and me.

He lifted two mugs from the table and was about to put them away when the other new girl spoke.

'Perhaps my colleague and I could have a drink of water?' She spoke with a kind of English accent, but there was a foreign sound to it too. I wasn't sure what 'colleague' meant.

'Help yourselves, girls,' said the man, putting the mugs back down. The girl whipped them off the countertop and filled them with water from the tap.

'My name is Karla,' she said, placing one of the mugs on the table in front of me.

'Hello, I'm Nancy.'

'Is that singing I hear?' asked Karla.

'It is,' said Miss Curran. 'Mr Niblock doesn't like us chatting when we're working, so one of the women asked him could she bring in her portable gramophone and play records. He said she could. So, we all end up singing; that's what's going on out there now.'

Karla and I sat quietly listening to the women talk about fashion, then move onto films they had seen in the cinema. I thought of Lilly when Miss Curran said how much she had enjoyed *The Keys of the Kingdom*.

We returned to our work to the tune of all the workers singing along with Gene Autry's 'Darling, How Can You Forget So Soon?' This was followed by the Andrews Sisters singing 'Rum and Coca-Cola'. One of the girls danced down the aisle with a pair of trousers over her arm. Karla and I laughed and joined in the bits we knew. She had a sweet singing voice. When a bell rang at one o'clock, Mr Niblock clapped his hands and called over all the workers.

'Just the women, please, for this announcement,' he said when some of the men moved over in front of him. They went back to their places.

'What I have to say will be short, but not very sweet. I have reason to believe that some of the women workers here have been talking to Miss Louie Bennett recently about joining that trade union for women, whatever it's called. I have been instructed by Mandel's to inform you that if you join the union, you say goodbye to your job here. Is that clearly understood?

'Yes, Mr Niblock.' All the women and girls were staring at the floor. I was thinking about Mona and what she might say if she heard this.

'And also note there will be no exceptions to this, no matter how long you have been with the firm. Off you go now for your break.'

Karla tapped my shoulder as we were walking out. She was wearing a royal blue beret.

'Care to go for a walk?' she said. The word 'walk' sounded almost like 'woke'.

'Where to?' I asked.

'Down to the quays. We could eat our lunch there.'

'You talk like an English girl,' I said.

'Good heavens,' she said with a little laugh. Her tongue licked her upper lip as if to check that her lipstick was still on.

'It's the way you say some words,' I said.

'That comes from having an English teacher for a mother,' she said, heading in the direction of the river. 'What do you think of the work so far?'

'It's easy. And you?'

'I was a bit disappointed to be employed as a runner. I was hoping to work on the machines. Do you like to sew?'

'I love it,' I said. 'My ma was great at sewing and my last teacher, Mrs Tierney, did a lot of it in school with us.'

'You said "was". Does your mother not sew anymore?'

'She died a few weeks ago. That's why Mrs Tierney helped me get the job.'

'Oh, I am sorry to hear that. Have I upset you by asking that question? Believe me, I wouldn't have asked had I known.'

'No, I'm used to telling people about it now. We'll be moving over to Leeds to my mother's aunt later on in the summer. That's where my father was from too.'

'*Was*?' asked Karla.

'He was killed in the war two years ago – fighting in Africa.'

Karla made a sound like 'tch' and shook her head.

'I am also sorry to hear that.' She slowed down and a flock of seagulls above us filled the grey sky with their cries. 'But at least he died fighting the Nazis,' she said, checking for traffic as we crossed the street. 'For that reason, he is a hero to me.'

I didn't think of Da as a hero. Nobody had said anything like that about him before. When he died, it seemed like a world away. I was upset for Ma, but I didn't think much about what it was like for Da out there. Karla calling him a hero made me wonder what it was like for him fighting the Germans in the desert. Was he scared? Did he think of us?

We were both deep in our own thoughts by the time we got to Custom House Quay. A couple of crates pulled together gave us a place to sit as we took out our sandwiches. Karla asked me about my brothers and sister. After that, I asked her about her family; she told me she had one younger sister called Vera, but quickly switched to talking about the Loreto Convent on St Stephen's Green; she had been at school there until the Easter holidays. I was surprised to find out that Karla was barely sixteen.

'Karla must study harder. She must read her books. She must write her essays. My head nearly went "boom",' she said, showing an explosion with her hands.

'So, you wanted to leave school?'

'More than anything! I was offered a job in a Jewish bakery at first.'

'A bakery,' I said, imagining the smell of fresh bread and sponge cakes. 'How did you say "no" to that?'

'For me that was easy. All I ever wanted to do was work at sewing. One of the Jewish ladies knew the Mandels and they agreed to take me on.'

'You're—'

'Jewish? Yes.'

'Are you from Germany?'

'No, but my mother is German. I'm from Czechoslovakia.'

Karla looked around. She stopped a man walking by and asked him the time.

'Time to go back,' she said. I knew by the way she was

walking that she didn't want to talk about where she was from anymore, so we both started talking about the style of dresses we liked. Karla used words I'd never heard of before, like 'scalloped necklines' and 'bertha collars'.

'Next door to the Rosenbergs lives a dressmaker,' she said, having explained what a 'basque waistline' was. 'I sometimes do a little hemming for her and she talks and talks about dresses and how she cuts and trims them.'

'Oh, I wish my mother could hear you. She would have loved all of that!'

'My friend also loves clothes and knows a lot about them.'

'Is she someone you were friends with in school?

'It's a he, not a she. I will tell you more about him another time.'

For the last few minutes of the walk, we didn't talk. I was going through all these new words in my head. I repeated them to make myself remember them. It was like learning a new language.

Chapter Ten

'Where's that boy gone?'

It was Wednesday morning in Mandel's and Miss Curran came running out of the office towards her table.

'He left ten minutes ago,' Mr Niblock answered.

'For where?'

'Merlyn Park, Ballsbridge – with Mrs Macken's order,' said Mr Niblock. 'Then I asked him to call out with another delivery to Mrs Delahanty in Booterstown, and two more on the way back.'

'Hmmph! We'll be lucky to see him back before we close,' said Miss Curran. 'You weren't to know that the delivery for the convent had arrived. I promised Mother Annunciata I would get it over to her straight away.'

'Why don't you ask the new girls to deliver it?' asked Mr Niblock. 'After all, we hired them as runners.'

'Excellent idea.' She scanned the room and stopped at me. 'Miss Kidd, you can leave that jacket until you come back. I need you to go on a message. Miss Popper, you can join her.'

She tapped the two parcels wrapped in brown paper, which were on her table.

'Take these to the convent in Sean MacDermott Street,' said

Miss Curran. 'Ring the doorbell and tell them you've a special delivery for Mother Annunciata. No need to wait for payment. The nuns will settle that with me at the end of the month.'

Karla took one of the parcels. I took the other one. We paraded across the floor towards the door.

'Some people have all the luck,' muttered Annie, the girl I recognised from school.

'Yeah, isn't it well for them not to have to listen to that high falutin' music,' said Jane beside her. I walked past as if I hadn't heard them.

Once we were out in the sunshine, Karla gave me a friendly dig in the elbow.

'Ah, what a relief to get out for a breath of air. I heard Mr Niblock say he was about to put some German opera music on the gramophone.'

'I didn't know *he* brought in records.'

'He hasn't before this, it would seem.'

'I can understand how German music would upset you.'

'Not because it's German, but because my mother loves opera, especially Schubert. The thoughts of hearing those arias she played so often on our gramophone in Prague—'

'Well, let's take our time going back. Maybe it'll be finished by then.'

We turned the corner into Buckingham Street, and a woman in a grey coat smiled as we came closer. She was wheeling a cart full of old clothes. A little black-and-tan terrier trotted behind her.

'Hello, girls,' said Mrs Hanlon. 'I've changed from flower seller to tugger today. Giving a bit of a hand to my sister.' I stopped to pet the little dog's head. Karla scratched the back of his neck. 'Is this a friend of yours, Nancy?'

'This is Karla. We're working together in Mandel's. This is Mrs Hanlon.'

'And who is this handsome little fellow?' asked Karla.

'That's Buttons. He's on loan from my brother out in Crumlin. On his holidays, the children keep saying.'

'You are looking after him for your brother?' asked Karla.

'More like my brother's looking after us by lending him to us! Buttons here is on a *working* holiday,' said Mrs Hanlon. 'He's been brought in to go after the rats. They're a curse down where we live. Isn't that right, Nancy?'

'He's on loan from your brother, you said?' I asked, pretending I hadn't heard the question. How embarrassing for Karla to hear about the rats in our house!

'He is, indeed. We're keeping him for one more night. If you've any bones, will you keep them for me?'

'I will, Mrs Hanlon,' I told her.

The pair of them continued down the street and we stood and watched them for a minute.

'He reminds me of Lenni,' said Karla.

'Your pet?'

'Yes. The sweetest little Dachshund, a gift from my grandmother in Prague. You never saw such a shiny brown coat as that little fellow had, and sad brown eyes and long droopy ears. He loved us all, but he 'specially loved my little sister Vera. Followed her around all the time … I should say until the law changed.'

'What do you mean?'

'A law was passed forbidding Jews to keep dogs.'

'Why would some people not be allowed to keep dogs?'

'I don't know. Nobody could explain it to me, but it meant Mama and Vera had to give Lenni away. One of our old neighbours took him.'

'Were they able to visit him at least?'

'No, a law was passed that banned Jews from that part of the city.'

'Did they ever hear anything about him after?' I asked.

'I do not know,' answered Karla. 'I have not had a letter from my mother since then. Since 6 September 1942, to be exact.'

No news in almost three years.

'That's hard,' I said.

'Their last letter came from Terezín – a concentration camp in Czechoslovakia.' We turned into Sean MacDermott Street. 'The Red Cross are trying to trace them. They're going through all the files—'

'Nancy Kidd! Are you mitching from school?' Lilly's voice called out from behind a pram being wheeled towards us.

'Could ask the same of you,' I said. 'I'm on a message to the convent.'

'From school?' asked Lilly, stopping in front of us.

'No, from work. I got a job. Started on Monday.'

'You're jokin'. And you never told me?'

'Never got a chance. Was going to tell you at Mass on Sunday.'

'Second Mass? Couldn't go. Ma said she wants a lie-in on Sunday anymore, so *she's* going to a later Mass over in Gardiner Street, and I've to stay and mind Imelda and the twins.'

'Mona wasn't there either.'

'Up all hours at a union meeting on Saturday night,' said Lilly. 'That Irish Women Workers' Union has taken over her life if you ask me. Where are you workin'?'

'Mandel's.'

'That place in Foley Street?'

'The very one.'

'Very fancy,' said Lilly in a put-on posh voice. In a dress too big for her, her hair brushed but in need of washing, she stared at Karla's neat blue beret and matching jacket.

'Lilly, this is Karla. She started the same day as me.' The girls nodded at each other.

'Meant to call over later on Sunday, but I'm busy—' I began.

'Don't talk to me about being busy,' interrupted Lilly

tetchily. 'I'm run off my feet lookin' after the twins.'

'Are they in the pram?' asked Karla, moving to get a look. Lilly pulled the pram back towards her to stop Karla looking in.

'They're at home. Both sick. Ma's with them,' said Lilly to me. 'Had to visit my uncle this morning.'

'Your uncle?' asked Karla pleasantly. She didn't realise that 'going to see your uncle' meant going to the pawnshop. Lilly had probably gone to Rafter's in Gardiner Street to pawn something from home to get badly needed money.

'Have to go home by number nine.' Lilly spoke to me as if Karla wasn't there and took off to cross to the other side.

'See you, Lilly,' I said. She didn't answer. If Karla had been able to look beneath the hood of the pram, she would have seen a covered can among the blankets. Lilly was on her way to the stew house in Buckingham Street to have it filled with stew for the family.

'Not very friendly, is she?' said Karla.

'She is when you get to know her,' I said.

We crossed the road at the convent. A queue of men stood beside the convent wall, some of them holding tin mugs. They were waiting to enter a door further down.

'What are those men lining up for?' Karla asked. I glanced over and spotted Sconsie third in the queue. I turned around quickly, hoping he wouldn't spot me.

'To get a mug of soup from the nuns,' I answered.

'One of them must know you. He is waving over at us.'

'Oh, probably mixing me up with someone else.'

I made sure to stand on the doorstep with my back to the line of men. What would Karla think of me, having the likes of Sconsie waving at me? We rang the doorbell of the convent and waited a few minutes. Nobody answered.

'I'll give it another ring. They mightn't have heard us the first time,' I said.

Within seconds, a tall scowling woman answered the door, wiping her hands on her apron. It was the convent housekeeper.

'Who do you think you are, ringing the doorbell twice?' she demanded.

'We thought—' I started.

'Thought, indeed! A little patience goes a long way, I always say! Come in.' She ordered us to enter a small hallway smelling of furniture wax and Brasso. A pair of highly polished double doors led into a corridor.

'Are you a penitent?' she asked, pointing her beak-like nose at Karla. 'If you are, I'll have Sister Xavier come and take your details.'

'I beg your pardon?' asked Karla.

'She isn't a penitent,' I said. 'We're not here about that. We've come from Mandel's with a delivery for Mother Annunciata.'

The woman took one more look at Karla, then turned her attention to the parcels.

'Oh, in that case, I'll take the delivery and make sure she gets it.

Before we had a chance to draw a breath, she scooped both parcels out of our arms and conducted us across the polished tiles back out to the street. The door banged behind us.

'Why did she ask if I was a "penitent"?' asked Karla.

'That's what they call the girls who work here.'

'Girls work here? What do they do?'

'Wash and iron clothes. There's a laundry at the back of the convent.'

'But "penitent" means they're sorry for something. What are they sorry for?'

'I think it's because they've caused trouble for their families. Girls who find themselves in the family way with no husbands sometimes come here because nobody will look after them.'

'Family way?'

'Expecting a child,' I whispered.

'And what happens to the babies?'

'As far as I know, they're brought to children's homes.'

'Children's homes?'

'Orphanages.'

'Ah, I understand. We have them in Czechoslovakia too. You know I always thought it peculiar to call a place an "orphanage" when so many of the children living in it aren't orphans.'

I had never thought about that.

We were walking along by the iron railings outside the convent, but Karla stopped and stared at the little black crosses on the top of the railings and shuddered.

'Those crosses ... they remind me of the ones the Nazi soldiers wore.'

I remembered seeing those black crosses on the uniforms of German soldiers when the newspapers printed photos of them. Karla looked the other way until we reached a gate with words in wrought iron above it.

'Monastery of Our Lady of Charity of Refuge,' Karla read. 'I see. It's a refuge for those girls. I wonder if this monastery of refuge will take refugees in after the war—'

I thought they wouldn't, but I didn't say anything. If I did, Karla would start asking more questions about the convent – questions that I wouldn't have a clue how to answer. Instead, I decided to tell Karla about Lilly and her family and how they were going through a very hard time.

'Ah, that explains why she wasn't so friendly,' said Karla. 'But this boy, Charlie? The brother? You like him?' she said, watching my face carefully.

'I suppose you could say I do,' I answered, and I couldn't help smiling.

Chapter Eleven

'No letter today,' said the postman on Saturday morning. I stepped into the hall when I heard him shouting different names at the door, hoping that mine would be among them. It was over two weeks since I'd heard from Aunt Gretta! It wasn't like her to wait this long. Maybe her hip was acting up and she wasn't able to post a letter. But I knew she had lots of good neighbours.

'Still no word, love?' asked Mrs McGee. She had heard voices in the hall and had to find out what was happening. I shook my head and slipped back into our kitchen.

Kate wasn't back yet from her Saturday cleaning job; Tom was out selling the papers; Patrick was playing with his little car on the bed. It was cool for the first week in May. I buttoned my cardigan as I headed down to Reilly's shop to buy a few messages.

Sconsie was sitting on the third step, drinking a cup of tea a neighbour had given him. I passed him by, hoping he wouldn't speak to me.

'It's a sorry sight when your neighbours don't acknowledge a good day,' he said as if he were talking to himself. 'I could swear it was yourself I saw over at the convent on Wednesday.'

Neighbours indeed. I had more to think about than whether or not I should have said hello to the likes of Sconsie. But when I thought about the buckets of water and how he had helped me, I did feel a little ashamed.

'Was on a message from work, Sconsie. Had no time to stop and talk,' I said, going out the door, but it sounded like what the teachers would call 'a poor excuse'.

I put Sconsie out of my mind and thought about what I was going to buy. Sugar and tea were on the list and my ration book was in my pocket. Mrs Reilly's huckster shop was the far end of the street. I opened the door and breathed in the familiar smell of fruit and vegetables, as well as the paraffin oil that was kept in a drum behind the counter. There were no customers and nobody serving, but the door into the kitchen was open and a chat was going on inside. One of the voices was Mrs Reilly's. Another belonged to a man, speaking with a culchie accent. The nasal tones of a third voice were a clear giveaway that the Pig Farmer was also in there. That wasn't unusual because she and Mrs Reilly were both members of the Legion of Mary.

'I'd better attend to my customers,' said Mrs Reilly. I could hear the sound of a chair being moved, scraping the kitchen tiles.

'Would you mind waiting just a minute, Mrs Reilly?' said the man. 'Tell me again, Mrs Knaggs, what time did you arrive in the shop?'

'Shortly after nine. I was coming in to get, to get … can't just remember now,' said the Pig Farmer.

'Don't worry about not remembering, Mrs Knaggs,' said Mrs Reilly kindly. 'The important thing is he was only five minutes gone when you arrived.'

There was other mumbled talk. While I waited, I studied the glass jars of acid drops, aniseed balls and satin pillows, on the shelves behind the counter. There were always empty jars among them, thanks to the shortage of sweets because of the war, but I ignored those and feasted my eyes on the colourful wonder of what *was* there. While I was imagining how delicious each of these would taste, something caught my eye – something lying on top of a sack of spuds under the window on my left. It was a boy's cap and it looked very like Charlie's. I moved closer to make sure. There was no mistaking it, the little check pattern of grey and black and the button on the top with a tear in the fabric. What on earth was it doing there? Charlie was never without his cap.

Something wasn't right about this. I moved sideways, pretending I was looking out the window. The people in the kitchen were very quiet. They could come out at any minute, so I had to act quickly, without making a sound. With my back turned towards the door into the kitchen, I grabbed the cap and slipped it under my cardigan. No sooner had it disappeared than a voice spoke behind me.

'Excuse me, young lady. What did you do, there?' The Pig Farmer spoke in her Holy Joe voice. I swung around.

'Nothing. I did nothing, Mrs Knaggs,' I said back to her. My face lit up.

'Then where's the cap that was there a minute ago?' she asked. A man appeared behind her. 'You saw the cap, didn't you?'

'I did,' said the thin-faced man, coming forward. He was wearing a long navy coat smelling of tobacco. As he pushed a pair of black-rimmed glasses up his nose, I noticed that the skin on his face looked tightly pulled over his cheekbones. 'It was there on that sack of potatoes.' He came out from behind the counter. Mrs Reilly followed him.

'I'd advise you to let go of your cardigan,' he said, hardly opening his mouth.

'You've no right to tell me what to do,' I said, but before I said another word, he pulled my hand away and Charlie's cap fell onto the bare boards below.

The man pounced on it and held it up in front of my face.

'Who does this belong to?' he asked, holding it so close to my face that it nearly brushed off my nose.

'I thought it was my brother's but I see now that it isn't,' I said.

'If you thought it was your brother's, why were you being so sneaky about it?'

'There was nobody in the shop. I saw it and thought I'd better take it home,' I said, trying to keep the quiver out of my voice. 'I made a simple mistake. I don't know what all the fuss is about.'

'Don't listen, Garda Greally. I wouldn't believe a word that comes out of that one's mouth,' said the Pig Farmer. 'This is the *child* I was telling you about. The one that's left in charge of three other children. Remember we saw the brother outside the Pro-Cathedral?'

'The Kidd children?'

'That's right. The family discussed at the last meeting.'

'The family Mr Sharpe is so concerned about. *You're* hardly the oldest, are you?'

I thought my stomach was going to drop onto the floor when I heard these words.

'I am,' I managed to say. I tried to stand as tall as I could but felt it made no difference. The man took a couple of strides towards the door and changed the 'open' sign to 'closed'. After a knowing nod to the women, he took a notebook out of his pocket and stood beside me, scribbling into it with a short red pencil that he whipped out from behind his ear. I remembered Ma had good time for Mrs Reilly. This was the time to say it.

'And I'm here to do my shoppin' 'cause Ma dealt here. Always had a good word to say about you, Mrs Reilly. Said you could be depended upon to be straight with your customers. You'll vouch for me, won't you?'

'Well,' said Mrs Reilly, adjusting the ribbons in her apron. 'I've always found the Kidds to be a decent family to deal with, but—' She looked at the Pig Farmer. 'I'd prefer not to get involved.'

Garda Greally checked his watch.

'I haven't much time. If you don't hurry up and tell me the truth, you'll have to come down to the station.'

'Go with you? Why should I?' I said.

'Do you hear the impudence of her?' said the Pig Farmer. 'That's what I've had to put up with all these years. Her late mother was the very same – stuck together with cheek.'

'Why should you go with me?' asked the guard. 'You might be more inclined to tell the truth about why you were sneaking away with this cap if I questioned you in the barracks.'

'I've explained—'

'Miss Kidd, I have years of experience of dealing with liars, so please don't insult me by repeating that fabrication. I'm sure you're aware of the Society for the Prevention of Cruelty to Children?'

'Yes, but—'

'They're already – how will I put it? – *concerned* about your family,' he said.

The Pig Farmer smirked at this, barely able to hide her enjoyment.

'It would be very easy for them to find you to be an

unfit guardian for your brothers and sister, and this certainly wouldn't help your case,' continued Garda Greally. 'Do you want your family to be brought before the Children's Court and sent away to industrial schools?' How could he talk so coldly about places such as Artane and Goldenbridge?

I was cross with myself for coming into the shop. For not turning around and walking out. For trying to take the cap. What on earth had Charlie done that all of this was going on? Then I thought of another way out.

'You can't do anything to our family,' I said. 'We're going over to my mother's aunt in Leeds.'

'Hmmph,' said the Pig Farmer. 'On what date are you leaving?'

'I don't have a date, but we are—'

'Whether you do or don't have a date doesn't make any difference,' said the guard, cracking his knuckles. 'The point is, you're in charge right now. If you're found to be an unfit guardian, you'll all end up being taken away. And mark my words, your sister and brothers would hold that against you for the rest of their lives. Look, we're giving you a way out. Simply tell me who owns this cap.'

'Why do you need to know?' I asked, trying to buy some time to think up a story.

'That's none of your concern,' said the guard. 'Now, tell us who owns this cap, or I'm going to march you down to the station.'

Think, think, think! I screamed in my head but no thoughts came. The mention of those awful places froze my brain. My knees started to shake. So much for being the brave girl Maggie admired.

'Well?' asked the guard, pushing his glasses up his nose again.

I couldn't bring myself to say his name.

'All right, a visit to the station might jog your memory.'

He took my arm. I shrugged it off; it struck me that if I was marched down to the station, everyone would know it was me who had told. I looked down at the floorboards.

'It's Charlie Weaver's,' I muttered.

Garda Greally scribbled a few more words into his notebook and snapped it shut.

'Good girl. Got that now. Important for evidence. Thank you, Mrs Knaggs,' he said to the Pig Farmer. 'And we'll report back regarding our investigation,' he said to Mrs Reilly. He snatched the cap up, stopped at the door to change the sign to 'open' and marched out.

I was left staring at the two women. Mrs Reilly went back in behind the counter.

'Now that's out of the way, what can I get you?' asked Mrs Reilly. I couldn't believe she was acting as if nothing had happened.

'Get me?' I repeated. Was she serious?

'What did you come in for, girl?' asked the Pig Farmer.

I looked at both of them. Did they honestly think I was going to buy something in the shop *now*?

'Nothin'. I came in for nothin',' I said and walked out.

'Are you all right, Nancy?' asked a kind voice as I was leaving the shop. A flowery perfume wafted from a black pram pushed by Mrs Hanlon.

'I'm fine, thanks.' She looked unconvinced.

'Skipped breakfast and feel a bit hungry is all that's wrong with me,' I said.

'Would you like me to wait for a few minutes – to make sure you're all right?' she said.

'No, but thanks all the same, Mrs Hanlon. I'll be grand.'

I walked on, keeping my eyes fixed on the windows of shops and houses. I couldn't bring myself to talk to anyone else.

'Did you get the messages?' asked Kate who was home and resting in Ma's chair when I came back into the house. She sat up and took another look at me. 'God, Nancy, what's happened?'

'Feel a bit sick. Had to come home,' I told her.

'Look, I'll get whatever we need,' said Kate. 'Give me the ration book and the money.'

'Don't go to Reilly's,' I said as I handed them to her, plus the scrap of paper where I had written down a few things.

'Reilly's? Why not?'

'Ma liked Mrs Reilly, but she's very friendly with the Pig

Farmer. The two of them are as thick as thieves in the Legion of Mary. Just don't feel I can trust her.'

'I always liked her, but if you feel that way, I'll head to Cregan's,' said Kate.

Once I had my cardigan off, I lay down on Ma's bed. There was something in that cotton cover that usually soothed me, but today nothing could calm me. The scene in the shop played again and again in my head. Me – the one always able to come up with a convincing story – had told on Charlie! What was going to happen to the Weavers now? But if I hadn't named Charlie, the Cruelty Men could be here now with a summons for the Children's Court.

Your first duty is to your own family, I told myself but it didn't make me feel any better. I closed my eyes. I felt like I was drowning in the shame of what I'd done. I dreaded the thought of meeting Lilly. She would be able to tell from me that something was up.

The door from the hall banged loudly, waking me with a start. Kate was back and here I was, lying on Ma's bed since she left. The scene in the shop, the cap, the name, the guard all barged into my brain. The shock of what happened must have sent me off to sleep. Now that I was awake, I wondered how I was going to hide the truth.

Chapter Twelve

On Monday at work, I couldn't bring myself to unwrap my sandwich at break.

'You are fretting because your aunt has not written?' Karla looked concerned.

'Yes, yes … I am worried. It's not like her,' I said, glad not to have to think up another reason for being out of sorts. 'I wish she'd write and let us know the date we're leaving.'

Though naming Charlie to the police hung over me like a thunder cloud about to burst, I was telling the truth when I said I longed for a letter from Aunt Gretta. It wasn't only about moving back to Leeds now; it was also a way to escape. If I could get away from Dublin, there might be some chance of turning my back on the past. I might be able to put Charlie's cap and betraying the Weavers into a box, stash it away in a part of my head, never to be opened again.

When I got home from work on Tuesday, I met Kate in the hallway with a bucket, on her way out to get water in the yard.

'Lilly's in there, waiting for you,' she said. 'Something's up but she wouldn't talk to me.' She stopped and whispered, 'It looks like something serious.'

'I'll talk to her,' I said, trying to make my voice sound calm. 'Take your time coming back.'

I paused outside the door, counted to three and walked in, hoping Lilly wouldn't notice the shake in my legs. She was sitting in Ma's old chair, staring at the fire. She never looked up, even when I dropped onto the chair across from her. Her eyes were bloodshot and her skin, usually pale and smooth, was covered in blotches.

'God, Lilly, what's happened?'

'The worst – the absolute worst,' she said.

'Is your ma all right?'

'She's not … because of Charlie.' She sniffed, trying not to cry.

I took off my jacket and threw it at the back of one of the chairs.

'Charlie?' I felt my heart thumping in my chest.

'That's right. Oh, Nancy, it's been terrible,' she said, biting her lip.

'I can make you a cup of tea—'

'No, I'm only here for a few minutes.' She stood up and walked over to the back window. 'Charlie's in big trouble.'

'Over selling the papers?'

'Yeah, but there's more. Money's been very tight over the last few weeks.'

'No wonder with your ma having to miss work there before

Easter when Imelda and the twins were sick.'

'That really set us back. Behind in the rent and all, we are. We've pawned anything worth pawning and sold the clothes coupons to some of the women at work.'

She sat down at the table.

'Couldn't go to any of my uncles – sure they're all strapped for cash, too. Same with my aunties. Ma already owes money to Mona and Bridie.'

'Why didn't you tell me, Lilly? We could've helped—'

'And your ma after dying?' said Lilly. 'It'd be the last thing we'd do. Anyway, Ma had to ask Charlie to lift some food in a couple of shops. We'd have had nothing to eat only for him!'

She swallowed and continued.

'Saturday morning, he stole some spuds in Mrs Reilly's but didn't she see him and try to stop him? On the way out of the shop, he pushed past her and his cap fell off.'

'And?'

'He got away, but the cap was left behind. Mrs Reilly reported it, but you know we don't deal with her, so she couldn't name him.'

'So, that's—'

'But she showed the cap to the guards. And this is the part that's hard to believe: they were able to get someone to say that the cap was Charlie's. Who would have done such a thing?'

She rested her head down on her arms on the table and,

thank goodness, didn't notice my blushes. What would she say if she knew the culprit was sitting across from her that minute?

'All the guards would say is that it was someone who knows the family well,' she went on.

'Where's Charlie now?' I asked, wishing that Kate would come back with the bucket of water so I wouldn't be sitting alone with Lilly.

'He's being held in Marlborough House, but tomorrow he's to be brought before the Children's Court.'

'And your ma?'

'At home, cryin' and lamenting. She's blaming herself for asking him to lift food in the first place.'

'Any chance he'll get off?'

'Between the Badge Man after him and now this, I doubt it,' said Lilly. 'And Ma is worried about the rest of us now. She's convinced the Cruelty Men are going to be there tomorrow to say she's an unfit mother.'

When I thought of Maggie's kind face and the way she looked after her family as best she could, I felt sick.

'Is there nobody to speak up for Charlie?' I asked.

'Not one. If Ma could afford a solicitor, that might help, but that'll be the day. Look, I've got to get back, but I wanted to tell you what happened.'

Kate appeared at the door with the bucket of water.

'All right to come in?' she asked.

'Yes, I'm leavin',' said Lilly.

She closed the door gently and I looked at Ma's chair. If only she were here to advise me what to do. But there was no Ma, Aunt Gretta was in another country, and now I wouldn't have Maggie to go to. How was I going to live this lie? How was I going to stand by and watch my best friend's family fall apart because of what I had done?

Kate placed the bucket of water in the corner.

'Thank God you didn't delay coming home from work. Poor Lilly. Something awful must have happened.'

'It did,' I said and I repeated Lilly's own words: 'The worst, the absolute worst.'

★ ★ ★

Those words haunted me that night and I dreamed that Lilly kept repeating them until I screamed at her that I knew what had happened. My eyes smarted as I went into work. Miss King took out the gramophone and placed a record on it. Frank Sinatra's voice singing 'Nancy (with the Laughing Face)' filled the room, and soon all the women were singing with it. Charlie had once told me that song always reminded him of me. As if that wasn't hard enough, Frank Sinatra had been Ma's favourite singer. Karla wasn't in that day, so during break, I walked the length of Buckingham Street and back to try to soothe my mind. The lyrics of that song pounded in my brain, especially the line about Nancy being like an angel. *Some angel I proved to be*, I thought to myself sadly.

That evening, I strolled towards Summerhill in the sunshine, but inside I felt dark clouds like you'd see on the wettest day in Dublin. Mrs McGee, Mrs Boland and Mrs Perrin were standing on the steps, close to each other.

'Ah, Nancy, such a sad business over at the Weavers,' said Mrs McGee.

'Poor Maggie. Lost the two lads four years ago, the husband last year and now to be faced with this,' said Mrs Perrin.

'I know only too well what she's going through,' said Mrs Boland whose oldest son, Ray, was in Artane.

'What happened?' I asked.

'Charlie was before Judge McCarthy this morning in the Children's Court,' said Mrs McGee.

'He's being sent off to Artane for shoplifting and selling the papers without a licence,' said Mrs Perrin.

'My brother-in-law, Mattie, works as a porter down there. He said when they led Charlie off in handcuffs, you'd hear the screams of Maggie in the Dublin mountains,' said Mrs McGee. 'And wasn't she put on warning about the rest of the children? The Cruelty Men are observing her, is what Mattie told me.'

'God help her if they are,' said Mrs Boland.

The thought of Maggie crying like that and Charlie being

taken off – I could feel the blood drain from my face.

'Nancy, love, are you all right?' Mrs McGee asked me. 'Ah, the poor girl, it's shocking for her to hear us talk and she a good friend of Lilly's. Will you come into my place and I'll make you a cup of tea?'

I knew Ma had no time for 'Busybody McGee', but the kind tone in her voice made me agree straight away and I followed her upstairs to her place – the back drawing-room.

'Clear those clothes away and sit down, love,' she said. There were two chairs and four or five orange crates that were used to sit on. I bundled the clothes off one of the chairs onto the window sill and sat down. Baby Jack, tucked up in one of Mrs McGee's shawls, was asleep in a wooden box beside me. Little Molly and Bernadette sat in the corner, tearing up some old newspapers.

'Boys, can you go and play outside for a bit?' she said to their brothers, Gerry, Paul and Pat. They saluted me as they took off out the door.

'See ya later, Ma,' called Gerry.

Mrs McGee climbed up on a wooden box to reach for something on a high shelf. 'This is where I keep my emergency supply of tea.'

She hung the kettle over the fire, and the paper-tearing game came to a sudden stop when Molly tried to pull a newspaper out of her sister's hand. Bernadette, on seeing how much

Molly wanted it, became all the more determined to hold onto it. Her grip tightened, her face reddened, and tears and shouting followed.

'Now, now, girls, will you give over with your fighting?' said Mrs McGee, plucking the newspaper from Bernadette's grasp. Both girls howled, but Mrs McGee passed no remarks. She made the tea and placed two cups on the table. By the time she poured the tea, the girls were leaning over one of the beds, talking to a little doll with a missing arm.

'Ah, poor Maggie,' she said. 'That woman's been through so much.' Jack had woken and Mrs McGee picked him up. 'My brother-in-law tried to calm her, but wasn't she crying that hard, she never heard a word.'

I tried to think of something to say, but all I could do was shake my head in sympathy.

'And the worst of it – the brother-in-law said – was that it was someone who knew Charlie that gave his name,' said Mrs McGee. She bounced a little on her chair to soothe the baby. 'You know – the day he was caught shoplifting in Reilly's?'

'Did they say who it was?' I asked, staring into my own cup.

'Indeed, they didn't. God help them if Maggie ever finds out who it is.'

'God help them is right,' I said, offering up that little prayer for myself.

Chapter Thirteen

I didn't see Lilly that evening, nor the next. I couldn't bring myself to go around. Supposing someone found out that I had given Charlie's name – after me stringing her along and pretending I didn't know. She'd never speak to me again. And if I told her myself? I couldn't see her talking to me after that either. Then there was Charlie finding out. What would he think of me if he knew? I couldn't bear to answer that question.

We had heard all about Artane from Mrs Boland upstairs. Her boy, Ray, was only ten when the school attendance officer had reported him for missing school – only a few weeks after his da died, too. Always a bit wild, he wasn't a month in Artane when he did a runner. They found him hiding in his auntie's garden in Cabra. The guards dragged him back, the Christian Brothers shaved his head, and all the boys watched as he was made stand on a chair while they beat him. The thought of that young fella, in bits after his father died, being beaten like that nearly made me sick when I heard it.

And then there were the Devanneys in number 48. When Mr Devanney fell ill and died, Mrs Devanney fell behind in the rent. The next thing was her three boys and only daughter were taken away from her. Wasn't up to looking after her children properly – according to the Cruelty Men. I can still remember her in floods when she was telling Ma one evening on the street.

'The three boys are sick and nobody's looking after them in Artane. Nobody will tell me anything!' she cried. 'As for Alice – she's in Goldenbridge, her fingers cut and sore from making rosary beads. When I complained to the nuns, she was moved to work in the laundry. Don't know which place is worse. Her arms are killing her from pulling those big heavy sheets out of the boilers with wooden poles. The poor thing won't stop crying to come home.' Three weeks later, Maurice, the oldest boy, died. The Christian Brothers told Mrs Devanney he had a weak heart. Mrs Devanney moved in with her sister in Crumlin and we never saw her again.

The memory of Maurice Devanney dying felt like a kick in the stomach. Supposing Charlie got sick … That thought had to be marched out of my head. Avoiding the family wasn't a good idea either. The very least I could do was to see if they needed any help.

On Friday evening, I worked up enough courage to call over to them in the Diamond. I was heading down the twenty-seven steps when I heard a voice behind me.

'Nancy Kidd!'

I turned around to see Mona, coming down the steps as fast as she could in a pair of black shiny high heels.

'Heading down to Lilly?' she asked.

'That's right.'

'I'll save you the bother by telling you that she's not in. Maggie and herself are working late.'

'Working?' I repeated.

'Did you not hear that Lilly started in the beads factory yesterday?'

So, Lilly had started in Mitchell's Rosary Beads Factory, where Maggie worked too.

'No – I wasn't talking to her since Tuesday. She didn't say anything about it then.'

'Since this business with Charlie happened, they don't know which end of them is up.'

'Poor Charlie,' I said, trying to keep the quiver out of my voice.

'It's like history repeating itself,' said Mona, leaning back against the wall.

'What do you mean?' I asked.

'You know – what happened to us.'

'What happened to you?' Lilly hadn't told me about anyone else in the family being sent to Artane.

'My big sister Lizzie stole from a house she was working in. Happened years ago.'

I knew Maggie and Mona came from a big family of seven girls and six boys.

'Lizzie was the second oldest of the family. Did Lilly never tell you?'

'No.'

'This was before I was born, mind, but Maggie told me all about it. God love Ma and Da. No matter how they tried, they couldn't feed all the children. To make matters worse, Ma was expecting Jeannie at the time. Lizzie took a few trinkets from the house to put food in their mouths and ended up in that place in Goldenbridge.'

'Ah, no, the poor thing. How old was she?'

'Thirteen, and if that wasn't bad enough, she was also a bed wetter. The first week she was there, the nuns made her march down the yard with her wet sheets for all the other girls to see.'

Aunt Gretta always spoke fondly of the nuns she knew and I remembered Granny did too. We didn't have nuns in the school in Rutland Street, but could they really have been that cruel?

'But Lizzie wouldn't do it,' Mona went on. 'Not one step would she take! Even when she was slapped, she wouldn't do it.'

'And what happened?'

'The nuns decided she was too much trouble and packed her off to the laundry in Sean MacDermott Street.'

'But I thought that place was for girls who … well … got into trouble – I mean in the "family way".'

'It is mostly, but other girls could end up there too.'

'Where is she now?'

'She died the week before she turned seventeen.'

'She died … I'm so sorry. That's awful.'

'Struck down by consumption. Had it goin' in and wasn't properly looked after. So, you can see why this brings back bad memories. Maggie was next to Lizzie, only two years younger. They were very close, the pair of them – so I was always told.'

'What about my ma? She'd have known about it.'

'That's right, but she was in Leeds when Lizzie died. Maggie told me how much she missed your ma that time.'

'No wonder Maggie's upset then. Charlie stole to help feed her and the others,' I said.

'And she's worried about his health in that place.'

This was more than I could bear to think about. I had to change the subject.

'Lizzie ... Elisabeth. Lilly's called after her?' I said.

'That's right. And I know *she's* in a bad way. She'll be glad to have a good pal like yourself, Nancy.'

'Well ... I do my best,' I muttered. 'Will you tell Lilly to call over to me tomorrow?'

'I will, and could you do something for me?'

'Sure, of course I will.' But I didn't feel sure of anything at that moment.

'Tell Lilly to join the union. Maggie left it when they had the strike there five years ago – some falling out she had with them – but Lilly needs the protection of a union. I tried to talk to her about it, but Maggie told me to leave her alone.' Then Mona took off down the steps as fast as those high heels would let her.

* * *

The next morning, Sconsie and Patrick gave me a hand carrying buckets of water in from the yard. The pot was on the fire, bubbling away. As the water heated, I poured it into the tin bath on the floor in front of the fire. I had the washboard and the packet of Rinso ready to go.

I had just put in my first lot of dirty clothes to steep when the door opened and in came Lilly.

'I'm getting the smell of the beads factory,' said Patrick, coming behind her with a bucket of water.

'No! I scrubbed myself before I came out,' said Lilly, putting her arm up to her nose and smelling it.

'It's from your hair,' said Patrick, sniffing at her.

'It's the smell of the cow horns. That's what they make the rosary beads from,' she told Patrick. 'So much for those caps, The women in the boiling house said to wear them to keep the smell off your hair.'

'Mona was telling me you'd started work,' I said.

'Had to with Charlie's money gone. The only job going was in the boiling house, so that's where they put me.'

'Are you going to join the union?'

'Mona was on to you?'

I nodded.

'I will, but not yet. Can't pay the fees for joining right now.

She knows how tight money is. Don't know why she keeps going on about it.'

'And how is Charlie?' Even saying his name made my stomach sick.

'Haven't seen him since. But Mrs Boland saw him when she was out visiting Ray.'

Lilly's voice had that forced sound of trying to be brave. She frowned at me and looked over at Patrick.

'Patrick, would you go down and call for Brendan, like a good lad?' I said.

'I want to know how Charlie is.'

'Doing as well as can be expected,' said Lilly. 'Now off you go.'

As soon as he had closed the door behind him, Lilly continued.

'We're not the better of it. He'd a black eye for starters – said he got it in a row with another lad. When Mrs Boland asked him how he was doing, he kept looking at the floor and just said, "Grand, grand".'

'Doesn't sound like Charlie,' I said, hoping Lilly wouldn't notice the redness in my face.

'Oh, Nancy, the thoughts of him in there for the next year. Ma is out of her mind with worry that he'll get sick and won't be looked after.'

'At least he'll get out after one year. Some boys have to spend several years in it.'

Lilly scowled at me.

'I don't care about other boys. All I care about is my brother,' she said.

'Mona was telling me about your Auntie Lizzie,' I said, trying to move away from the subject of Charlie in Artane.

'Someone you never heard me talk about,' said Lilly. She had her 'haughty' look on, still sore with me for talking about other boys.

'That's true…'

'It upset Ma whenever we asked about her, so Charlie and me steer clear of mentioning her. Same way we don't talk about Raymie and Larry.'

'And how is your ma now?'

'We're managing but—' She paused to swallow, then continued. 'One of the Cruelty Men was sniffing around the day before yesterday. Asking questions about Ma, Imelda and the twins and me.'

I could feel my mouth go dry when she said this.

'Your ma does such a good job.'

'That's what we thought about Mrs Boland and Mrs Devanney,' said Lilly. 'And look what happened there.' If only she knew how much I had thought about Ray Boland and Maurice Devanney of late.

I dragged the wet clothes onto the washboard. Lilly watched me.

'What about you?' she asked. 'How's work?'

I welcomed the chance to talk about something else. I told her all about Mandel's – the work I did and the way we sang with the gramophone records.

'We sing sometimes, too,' said Lilly. 'It helps to make the time go faster.' We chatted about the songs for a few minutes. Then Lilly looked at the clock.

'Have to go, but tell me first, are *you* going to join the union?'

'No unions allowed there. If you join, you get the sack,' I told her.

'That's no way to treat the workers,' said Lilly, and she sounded so much like Mona, I almost smiled.

'Any word from your aunt in England?' She pushed the chair back into the table.

'No word,' I said. 'To tell you the truth, I'm a bit worried. It's not like her to be this quiet. If I don't hear from her by next Saturday, I'm writing to *her*.'

'Good idea.'

'I'll be out with you. I've got to look after Sconsie for helping me with the water.'

I took a mug of tea and some fancy bread and walked into the hall with Lilly.

'There you are, Sconsie,' I said, and he sat down on the third step, all smiles.

Mrs McGee heard us and was down the stairs in a flash.

'How are you all managing?' she asked Lilly.

'We're doing the best we can,' said Lilly, not stopping. 'Haven't much choice, have we?' she added in a whisper to me, as she hurried out the front door.

Chapter Fourteen

Karla and I were on first break. Making our way towards the kitchen, we passed Mr Niblock, examining a docket at his desk. He looked up and said something to Karla in a foreign language, and she answered. When he spoke again, his voice sounded different – gentle and kind.

'What language were you speaking?' I whispered to Karla as we sat down at the table.

'German. Like me, his mother is German,' she whispered back. 'He was asking if I'd had news of my family.'

Johnny Quinn stood with his back to us at the sink, filling the kettle with water. Jane and Annie were huddled together at one corner of the table. Jane looked up.

'We were just talking about you, Karla. Do you still have family beyond?'

'Beyond what?' asked Karla.

'Beyond in Prague,' Jane said. Karla hesitated.

'Don't tell me they ended up in one of those dreadful places,' Jane continued. 'What are they called, Annie?'

'Camps, I think they call them,' said Annie, stuffing a sandwich into her mouth. 'Why they call them camps is beyond me.'

They both sat and looked at Karla. She opened her mouth to say something then closed it.

'There was a lot of reading about those places in the papers over the weekend,' said Johnny, placing the kettle on the cooker to boil. 'The missus and meself couldn't believe what went on in them. And isn't it good enough that Hitler and his cronies got their comeuppance in the end?'

'Pity they didn't get it a lot sooner,' I said, taking out some cups and putting them on the table.

'But what about your—' started Jane again, looking at Karla.

'Some things are very hard to talk about,' I said, frowning at the pair of them.

'And very private,' added Karla, putting out some teaspoons.

'Excuse me,' said Jane. 'I was only making polite conversation.' For the rest of the break, she sat with what Ma used to call a sourpuss, and never opened her mouth. Johnny and Annie started to talk about a woman they both knew from Mary's Mansions. Karla nodded at me to go out to the corridor. We had a few minutes left.

'Miriam, who used to live close to us in Prague, has been to the Red Cross office three times this week, but still no news.'

'Oh, I hope you hear something back very soon,' I said, trying to imagine what it must be like not knowing if your mother and sister were alive or not.

When we returned to the workroom, 'Roddy McCorley'

was playing on the gramophone – one of my favourite songs from school. Every time it came to the line 'And young Roddy McCorley goes to die—' Karla joined in, and we both sang loudly.

I was bringing a pair of trousers over to be checked by Miss King when something caught my eye at the window. I looked over.

It was Jemmy and Mickser. The music could be heard outside and there was the pair of them marching in front of the window. Jane and Annie tittered. I kept my head down, hoping they wouldn't notice me, but Mickser banged at the window and waved. I looked around, pretending to wonder who he could be waving at, but alas, he started calling my name, and the music wasn't loud enough to drown his voice.

Miss Curran walked in front of me.

'Get rid of that pair, this instant!' she whispered as she passed.

I tried to get up and go to the door without making it too obvious, but Loretta Madigan, the prettiest, best-dressed girl in the factory, was on her way back from the kitchen and nodded towards the two boys.

'Friends of yours?' she said, making sure the girls nearby heard her.

I ignored her and stepped outside.

'Would you look at who's graced the street with her presence?' said Mickser.

'Are you trying to get me fired?' I said, almost in tears.

'Oh no, are we upsettin' you?' said Mickser in mock concern. 'We'd better go away. Will we go away, Jemmy?'

'We will, Mickser,' said Jemmy.

Mickser looked around and lowered his voice.

'But it'll cost you. Give us threepence and you'll be rid of us.'

'Don't have any money on me,' I whispered. 'Will you leave me alone! Bad enough that you were forcing my brother to buy a pup off you,' I said to Mickser.

'I'm sure you've got some change inside.'

'I'm not going in for any money.' The thoughts of parading through the workroom and out again filled me with horror.

'Sure, let's go back to the window then,' said Mickser. 'We're happy to continue entertaining your friends. Aren't we, Jemmy?'

'We are, Mickser. *And* we're happy you no longer have Mr Charlie Weaver around to fight your battles,' added Jemmy.

They started walking slowly back towards the window. A woman in a smart green tweed suit approached the door to go in. I moved to one side as she looked over her shoulder at the two boys and scowled. I felt that if my face turned any redder, my cheeks would explode. What could I do to get rid of them? As if my prayer was answered, a voice came from behind me.

'You must be Mickser and Jemmy.' It was Karla.

'Yeah, so what if we are?' asked Mickser.

'A couple of the girls inside were able to identify you.'

'*Identify* us. Do you hear that?' said Mickser.

'It's not Scotland Yard you're working for. *Identify* us! I'm all of a tremble,' said Jemmy.

'Ah, please do not tremble, boys. Because I have goodness in my heart, I have come out to warn you that Mr Niblock is on the phone to the police about you this very minute.'

'Over what? We're not doing anything,' said Jemmy.

'You are harassing people in their workplace. That's against the law.'

The two boys looked in the window and, sure enough, Mr Niblock was on the phone.

'She's right, Mickser,' said Jemmy. 'I'm not hanging around!' And he took off running down the street. Mickser looked at Karla, trying to think of something clever to say, but none of his usual smart words came. He hightailed it down the street after Jemmy.

'Who was able to identify them?' I asked Karla as we watched them.

'Nobody. I was standing at the door and heard the names. Mr Niblock said he was calling a supplier, so I pretended that he was on the phone to the police.'

'And that law about harassing people?'

'Made up. Sounded very convincing, no?'

'Totally convincing. You're wasted here,' I said.

'What do you mean?

'You should be on the stage,' I said. 'Come on. Let's go back in.' Then I stopped. 'I feel a bit embarrassed to tell you the truth. People heard those two call me by my name.'

'Psshh!' said Karla. 'Everybody in the workroom is back thinking of their own work and singing about some man called Roddy McCorley. Do you think they're worried about Nancy Kidd and the two boys out on the street?'

She grabbed my arm just before we went into the workroom.

'What was that one of them said about Charlie not being around anymore? That's Lilly's brother, isn't it?'

'He got into trouble,' I whispered, not looking at her. 'Ended up in Artane.'

'Artane?'

'I'll explain later.'

I would tell her about Charlie, but not my part in it.

As we walked back to our tables, Miss Curran shook her head as if to say, 'Never let that happen again.' I nodded to her and got straight back to work.

Chapter Fifteen

On our break the following day, we strolled along the footpath towards the Liffey. That meant we could talk without others listening in. Karla was asking me about Artane.

'So, Charlie was sent to this dreadful place for stealing a few potatoes and selling newspapers without a licence? How long will he be there?'

'For a year. He'll be let out on his sixteenth birthday.'

'Will you be able to visit him?'

I longed to see Charlie, but the thought of visiting him in that place … I didn't think I had the nerve to do it.

'I'm not sure about that, Karla,' I said. She was getting ready to ask me more questions, but I wanted to change the subject and got in with a question of my own: 'Any news about your mother and sister?'

'Yes. I received a letter from Miriam, our old neighbour. She said the Red Cross records show they were in Terezín in January. She said not to give up hope: people are turning up all the time. But it's hard. It's so hard.'

Here I was, feeling sorry for myself. What was it like for Karla, not knowing if her mother and sister were alive?

'What was it like to live in Prague?' I asked, wanting to remind her of happy times.

'If you are asking about my old life – it's like talking about another world. Our home was in a beautiful part called Letná.'

'Did you live in a house or a flat?'

'A flat – a big one, full of old furniture that my grandmother had left us. There was a sunny courtyard out the back, and when we looked out the window, we could see the trees in the park.'

'A park?'

'Yes – a public park. My mother used to bring my little sister Vera and me to walk in the park every day after school. She spoke English to us, and German.'

'German?'

'Remember I told you my mother was German. She came from Dresden and taught English at Charles University – that's in Prague – up until the time she got married.'

'She's Jewish – like your father?'

'Yes, but we were not a religious family. We sometimes celebrated feast days such as Passover with my aunt and our cousins, but in our own home, religion was never discussed.'

We walked for a little bit.

'The year I left – that was 1939 – my father used to read out pieces from the newspaper about what Hitler was doing in Austria. My mother always said, "That will never happen here." But things were changing in Prague. One morning I went into school and two girls in my class held their noses as I passed in the corridor. They made a remark about "smelly Jews". When I told the teacher, she shrugged her shoulders and said nothing.'

'What? Didn't say anything to them?'

'Not one word. But things got much worse. I will never forget the day the German army marched into Prague. It was Wednesday, 15 March, a freezing morning and snowing too. Even with snow on the ground, we could still hear their boots as they paraded down our streets. The sight of them in their helmets and their iron crosses—'

'Did Czechoslovakia not have an army? Why didn't they go out and stop them?'

'Everybody was too afraid; their army was so big and powerful. But there was one brave group of people in my country. They worked – how do you say it? – "behind the scenes". They were called the "Resistance Movement". They made life as difficult as possible for the Germans.'

We stood at the wall on the quays and she looked into the river.

'But life for us would never be the same. "Jews are forbidden to walk in the following streets. Jews are forbidden to live in the following areas. Jews are forbidden to enter the following parks." Even our lovely park beside us was out of bounds.'

'But I thought you said you weren't religious.'

'We weren't, but that didn't make any difference. We were Jews and that was all that mattered. Then my father got a notice that he was no longer allowed to work as a doctor. What a blow that was for the poor man.'

'What did he do?'

'He got a job filing in a newspaper office, but one night he was called out to work as a doctor. It was to look after a man who had been working for the Resistance. He had been beaten up by the Gestapo.'

'What's the Gestapo?'

'The German secret police. After that, Papa often was called on to help, but one night, when he came back home, there were two German police officers waiting for him at our door, to arrest him.'

'For what?'

'They would not say.'

'What happened to him?'

'We did not find out for a long time. My mother asked at the police station every morning. Every time she was told that Papa's actions proved him to be an enemy of the state.'

Her voice got softer.

'After they took him, his bank account was frozen. We were forced to sell the furniture from our apartment. Because we were Jews, people gave us very little money for it. Soon after, we had to move to the other side of Prague where we shared a four-roomed apartment with three other families. Life was so different then. The three of us and our little dog Lenni all ate and slept in one bedroom. Vera and I had to go to a different school. My mother was tired all the time and cried over my father. She started speaking English to me every chance she got. I will always remember the day she sat me down at our little table and told me that she had arranged for me to go to a Jewish family in London. I was to leave on 2 August. There was only one place and, being the older girl, I was to go. She promised that once all her affairs were in order, she and Vera would join me.'

'Who was going to bring you to London?'

'An Englishman called Nicholas Winton. He had been bringing children out of the country for months, and my mother felt she could trust him. In London, a man called Max Rosenberg and his wife Irma were willing to take me in.'

We were still standing at the wall beside the Liffey and she peered into the water again.

'The evening that I was leaving, Mama brought Vera and me for a special ice-cream in Wenceslas Square. I'm sure it cost a lot of money that she could not afford. We waited on the platform as the Englishman rounded all us children up and put us on the train. I thought it was all a great adventure until I saw Mama crying when the train was pulling off.'

She stopped and bit her lip to stop herself crying.

'The look on her face as we moved away – it still haunts me. It was the face she cried with over Papa. That was the last time I saw her.'

Karla patted her beret and swallowed.

'Remember I told you about the last letter from Mama in September 1942? That was the letter that told me about Papa. A telegram had come saying that he had died in Auschwitz.'

'Isn't that one of those concentration camps?'

She nodded. 'And of course, Mama and Vera were in Terezín at that time.'

I thought about what was being said about those places and shuddered.

'What happened after you got on the train?'

'We travelled all night, and sometime during the next afternoon, we crossed the border into Germany. We all had to get out. Our bags were checked and the border police took whatever they wanted from our luggage and kept it for themselves. The train took us across Holland next. By the evening time, we had reached the Hook of Holland.'

'Had you anything to eat?'

'Yes, we had all brought some food and we shared what we had. The sea crossing was awful. I was sick all the time. Then we arrived at Harwich and got a train from there to London.'

'Was that family there to meet you?'

'Yes, Max and Irma were there and off I went with them in their car to Stamford Hill. They had a baby boy called Joshua. Five weeks later, Britain declared war on Germany. Irma was very nervous, so they decided we'd be safer in Dublin where Max is from. Luckily his brother owned a house that we could move into.'

'In Camden Street?'

'That's right. I went to Zion National School first, then I was almost three years in the Loreto Convent.'

'I know you said you didn't like school but I'm still surprised you left.'

'That's the worst thing about being a doctor's daughter. All of the teachers expected me to be smart and very willing to learn, but I found school very difficult. I felt restless all the time, and most of the lessons were boring.'

'Did you have to do Irish?' I asked.

'No, I didn't do Irish or religion. I was expected to study during that time. But although some of what I read went in here,' she said, pointing to her forehead, 'I'm sorry to say it soon departed! Not like my friend Levi. He's studying to be a doctor.'

'Levi? That's an unusual name.'

'Not if you're Jewish. He's also from Prague. His father and Papa were colleagues.'

'What does "colleague" mean?' I asked, remembering that she had used the word when we first met at Mandel's.

'Someone you work with.'

'Did he come over with you?'

'No, he left the year before me for London.'

'Is he older than you then?'

'Oh yes. He is twenty-three now. Remember I told you I had a friend who loves clothes and knows a lot about making them? That's him.'

'I thought you said he was going to be a doctor?'

'He is, but he spent a year working in a clothes factory in London to learn English before he started in college.'

'When did he come to Ireland?'

'Back in 1940 – remember all those people moving out of London because of the Blitz? He came to Dublin then and continued his course in Trinity College. He has to go back to London once the war is over. His work permit only allows him to be here until then.'

'Do you see him often?'

'Most weeks. He works part-time for Eppenstal's, driving the delivery van.'

I wondered if Levi was Karla's boyfriend.

'And what about the Rosenbergs? What are they like?'

'Max and Irma? They are good people, but they had a new baby a month ago. That's their third child, so space is very tight.'

'What did they say when you told them you wanted to leave school?'

'They reminded me that the Dublin Hebrew Congregation was paying my school fees and that lots of girls would love to be in the position that I was in. I told them the money would be better spent on a more deserving student and that I was happy to start working and contribute to the rent.'

'They gave in then?'

'It took a while! In the meantime, that job I told you about had come up at the bakery, and then Mandel's.'

That night, Karla was on my mind. She had lost so much during the war and didn't even know if her mother and sister were alive. There was hardly room for my own worries in my head – or so I thought. But like a stain on a white shirt that can never be scrubbed away, my own worries were still there, and when they wormed their way back into my thoughts, they weren't in a hurry to leave anytime soon.

Chapter Sixteen

On the following Saturday morning, I had finished washing the clothes and had the rags and a bucket of soapy water ready to clean the kitchen, when someone gave a loud knock on the door.

'Registered letter for Miss Kidd,' said a voice outside. The postman smiled. 'You've got your letter at last,' he said as I signed for it.

'That's strange,' I said to Patrick, back in the kitchen. 'A letter from Aunt Gretta, but why would she need to register it? Maybe it's a postal order to help with the rent.'

I opened the envelope carefully, took out several sheets of paper and began to read it to myself:

16 Neville Road

Leeds 9

Dear Nancy,

I know it's been a while since you heard from me; that's because I heard news of an alarming nature which I had to get used to before I could take up my pen to write to you.

When I called to your grandmother in Leeds to tell her the news about your mother, she took out that photo to send to you. As she was handing it to me, she made some comment about your mother. I thought I had misheard her and asked her to repeat it. She said she often wondered who Esther's real parents were. When she saw how shocked I was, she said she thought I knew that when your mother was getting married, she had to get her birth certificate from Dublin. That's when she found out that my sister did not give birth to her.

I was so taken aback that I wrote to Mrs Knaggs, an old neighbour of ours and at one time a great friend of my sister's. As you know, she and your Granny fell out years ago. I knew it had to be something very serious because those two had always been best pals. When they parted – neither of them ever to give in – it always puzzled me.

Mrs Knaggs was indeed able to confirm what I had heard from your grandmother in Leeds, and I feel it's unfair that it has fallen on me to tell you, but tell you I must. This is the account I was given: In 1911, a girl was brought by her family to the Magdalen Laundry in Sean Mac Dermott Street. She was in the family way but was also behaving very strangely. She refused to talk to anyone and kept trying to escape. After she gave birth to a baby girl, her behaviour got worse. She kept running away, and when she was caught, not only would she refuse to speak, but she kept closing her eyes and refusing to look at anyone. The nuns couldn't cope with her and had her committed to the mental hospital in Grangegorman, where she died soon after. Honora heard that the baby girl was going to be sent to an orphanage. God didn't bless her with a child of her own, so she persuaded her husband that they should take her. Mrs Knaggs, being a close friend back then, strongly advised her <u>*not*</u> *to take on this child – that it would very likely inherit the waywardness of the mother. But my sister always had a stubborn streak and was deaf to good advice. An unmerciful row followed and they never spoke again.*

It grieves me sorely that Honora and her husband took advantage of the fact that I was over in Leeds to keep the truth from me. Remember I told you about those five years I spent as a nun before I took up my position as a housekeeper? That time was spent in an enclosed order of sisters, and we weren't allowed any letters from home. When I finally left the convent, my sister wrote to tell me she had a four-year-old daughter called Esther, and she was now a widow as Joe had been killed in France during the war.

Although I was fond of your mother and found her to be a good worker, I was against her marrying your father at such a young age. Would she listen to me? Not a bit. But at the time, I considered her my own flesh and blood and was prepared to overlook the folly of youth.

Which brings me to the point of this letter. I've sent you money to pay for your mother's funeral and that's the last help you'll get from me. I cannot begin to tell you how hurt and angry I feel at being deceived all this time. As we clearly are not family, your coming here is out of the question. I have been duped for years, and now that I know the truth, I feel obliged to act on it. Please do not write to me in the future. I will no longer be at my old address as I am moving in with my friend, Mimi.

Yours sincerely,
Gretta McDaid

'Well, what's it about?' asked Patrick. 'Did she send a postal order?'

'She's advising about this and that. You know Aunt Gretta! I'll read it again to myself later when I've the cleaning finished,' I said, folding up the pages quickly and slipping them into the pocket of my skirt. The letter may as well have been one of the Guinness cart-horses trampling over me. I moved over to the dresser and started taking down Granny's china so that I could dust and clean the shelves. I had to mull over the letter and decide how to tell the others. The pain of losing Ma flared up. I placed half a dozen saucers on the table. She'd have had half a dozen canaries if she knew that Tom had joined the newsboys, but how would she have been about this letter? I could only imagine how angry she'd have been after reading it. Not angry – *furious*! We'd have all been annoyed and upset but you could depend on Ma to lead the charge and know the best way to handle Aunt Gretta.

'All right, Nancy?' asked Patrick.

'All right. Just a bit tired.'

I needed to talk to somebody. Fr Gill, the parish priest, maybe? He was a kind man, but something stopped me from going to him. I wasn't sure what. Somehow, I felt that he wouldn't understand how awful it was for us to get this letter. If he wasn't the right person, who was? Mrs McGee? Every last person in Summerhill would know about it by nightfall if I told her. The more I thought about it, the clearer it became to me who the right person was. That afternoon, I called over to Lilly's.

'Is your ma in?' I asked her.

'Everything all right?'

'No.'

'God, Nancy, what's happened?'

'A letter.'

'From?'

'Aunt Gretta.'

Lilly was going to ask another question but stopped herself.

'I can see by the look of you, it's a ma you need to talk to,' said Lilly. 'Come on in. She's next door in Mrs Casey's with Imelda and the twins. I'll give her a shout.'

She went over to the window, opened it, put her head out and shouted: 'Ma, you're wanted!'

'Who is it, love?'

'Nancy. She's come over specially to talk to you.'

Maggie's voice came back. 'Tell her I'm comin'.'

Her first words on coming into the room were to Lilly: 'Make us a cup of tea, love.'

'Are you sure, Maggie?' I said, given tea was rationed.

'Of course, I'm sure. If I'm not mistaken, this looks like a situation where tea *has* to be taken. Think nothing of it.'

I sat down on one side of the table and showed Maggie the

letter, while Lilly scalded the cracked brown teapot.

'Do you mind if I read it out, Nancy, so Lilly will know what's in it?'

I told her to go ahead and she read it aloud, adding sighs and 'tut-tuts' at different points.

'I never heard the likes,' said Lilly, measuring tea-leaves to add to the pot.

'Did Ma ever tell *you*, Maggie?' I asked.

'Not a word,' said Maggie.

'And I can't believe she never told us,' I said.

'No doubt she kept it to herself because she didn't want to upset Mrs Murphy – I mean your granny. She was probably going to tell you at some stage. What I can't believe is how Gretta's letting it change everything. It's not like she didn't know your ma or the rest of yiz.'

'That's what I can't understand either,' I said. 'It's almost as if she's blaming *us* for not being told the truth.'

Lilly filled the teapot with boiling water. 'It must be a shock to find out you have a granny you never knew about.'

'It is, but to tell you the truth, the way Aunt Gretta took the news is more of a shock,' I said.

'She doesn't see that you're as innocent in all of this as she is,' said Maggie. 'Those old secrets that families keep! They've a habit of worming their way out and causing a lot of heart-break and upset when they do.'

'Like Aunt Lizzie in our family,' said Lilly softly, pouring out three mugs of tea.

'But I never kept her a *secret*. I heard Mona was telling you about her.' Maggie scratched the back of her neck. 'Ma and Da never talked about her at home. Their way of thinking was talkin' about it brought back sad memories. When it came to having my own family, I sort of did the same. Lar and myself – we didn't talk about Raymie and Larry. If we did, it'd all come flooding back.'

She made the sign of the cross. I watched Lilly take the jug of milk out of the basin of cold water and add some to the tea. She glanced at me. This was a rare mention of her two brothers.

'What about your da's ma?' said Maggie. 'Would you think of writin' to her?'

'Nanny? You heard Ma giving out about her often enough. We hardly ever saw her when we lived in Leeds. She never really cared about us.'

Maggie stirred her tea.

'Is there anyone we could ask to talk to your Aunt Gretta first?'

'What about Fr Gill?' I suggested. 'Aunt Gretta used to work as a priest's housekeeper. I'm sure there's a number he could call and talk to her.'

'That's a great idea. If she heard your side of the story from Fr Gill, she might see things differently. She has great respect for priests. Have a word with him after Mass. He could be the one to turn things around for you.'

She smiled and put her arm around me.

'But as long as you're still livin' in Dublin, you've got to be very careful. The Cruelty Men will be watching you. "Are you able to mind the family?" they'll be asking. They wouldn't think twice about dragging you to the Children's Court and sendin' you off to Goldenbridge and Artane.'

'We should know,' said Lilly. 'They've been snoopin' around here, often enough.'

'And I hate to have to remind you but it has to be said: be careful of the Pig Farmer. She's one of their informants.' Maggie picked the letter up off the table and handed it back to me. 'The fact that she has a grudge against you makes things even worse. It's a mystery to me why she holds on to that old grievance. Your granny didn't follow her advice years ago and she's *still* sore about it?'

I thought about the letter and the way Aunt Gretta described Granny and the Pig Farmer as 'pals'. *Some pal,* I thought.

I remembered the Pig Farmer's smug grin on the day I'd snitched in Reilly's shop. She had received Aunt Gretta's letter by then. She knew more about what was going on than we knew ourselves.

'And one last thing, Nancy,' said Maggie.

I stopped.

'If Fr Gill talks to your aunt, will you let me know how it goes?'

'You'll be the first to know,' I said, heading out the door. Mona was on her way in. She saw the letter in my hand.

'You've heard from your aunt at last?' she said, smiling. 'When are yiz off to Leeds?'

'I'm not sure,' is all I managed to say.

'I'll fill you in,' shouted Lilly from inside.

Mona looked kindly at me.

'Ah, take care, Nancy,' she said softly, patting my shoulder.

* * *

On Sunday evening, I stood on the doorstep of the parochial house on Killarney Street.

'Is Fr Gill in?' I asked the housekeeper. She hadn't seen me since Ma died, and she grabbed my hand and whispered, 'Sorry for your trouble, love.' She brought me into the front parlour. I sat on an armchair at the side of the fire, but even with a crocheted cushion behind my back, I could not feel at ease. A big painting of the Flight into Egypt hung over the mantelpiece. The door opened and a voice spoke.

'You're surprised to see me, Nancy. I know you were talking to Fr Gill this morning after Mass and he asked you to call back this evening,' said Fr Comiskey.

'That's right, Father. Did he get to talk to Aunt Gretta, do you know?'

'He had so many parishioners to visit in hospital today, I asked him if I could do it.'

'And you talked to her?

'I did.'

'And what did she say?'

'I described your family situation, the way you were all ready to move. I tried to reason with her about the new information she was given.'

'And?'

'I'm afraid she won't change her mind.'

I felt a surge of panic in my stomach.

'I tried my best to talk her 'round,' continued Fr Comiskey. 'But there's no going back for her. She's going to move to Whitby – to live with an old friend of hers. She's selling up the house in Leeds.'

'As if she never knew us,' I said. 'I can't understand it.'

'It's the shock of finding out the truth. It has affected her badly.

'But doesn't she know it's a shock to us, too?'

'I told her that, Nancy, but she wouldn't listen.'

'I thought she knew us and, well, loved us enough. If she did, none of this would matter.'

'Yerra, it's the old way of thinking,' said Fr Comiskey.

'What do you mean, Father?'

'Miss McDaid firmly believes that whatever ailed your grandmother affected your mother and affects you, her children.'

My grandmother? It took a moment to realise that he was talking about the woman who gave birth to Ma, the girl in the Magdalen Laundry.

'Your grandmother had no husband and had a mental affliction. Miss McDaid thinks that your mother was tainted with the same blood.'

'What has that to do with us?'

'Sadly, she thinks the next generation has – shall we say – inherited the same tainted blood.'

'*Tainted*? Blaming us for things that happened years ago – before we were even born?' I said.

'I tried to point out that it wasn't how Christ would have behaved,' said the priest.

'And what did she say?'

'It pains me to tell you, but I think you need to know the truth. She repeated what she said to you in your letter: you're not her blood relations and she no longer feels responsible for you.'

This wiped out what little hope I had been clinging onto. Fr Comiskey picked up a prayer book from a polished table beside his chair and made circles with his thumb on the leather cover. There was a knock on the door.

'Excuse me, Father,' said the housekeeper. 'You're wanted on the telephone.'

'I have to go now, Nancy. I'm sorry my conversation with Miss McDaid did nothing to change her mind.'

'I'm sorry too, Father,' I replied. What else could I say?

Chapter Seventeen

Karla always had her hair brushed nicely, always wore lipstick, always dressed smartly, but on Monday morning she rushed into Mandel's looking as if someone had dragged her through the streets of Dublin.

'Are you all right?' I whispered to her as she passed by my table.

'See you outside at break?' she answered.

She walked towards her table, but Mr Niblock called her into the office. It was a good half-hour before they both emerged and, head down, she slouched back to her place. I glanced over several times, but she was intent on her work and looked to be in her own little world.

Break came at last. Karla almost ran out of the building and I hurried after her. Once we were out on the footpath, she tried to say something, but a sob choked the words. She covered her face with her hands.

'Did something happen at work?' I asked. 'I saw you go into the office.'

'No, work is fine.'

'Is it your mother and sister?'

She shook her head.

'Did you have a row with Levi?'

She took out her hankie and dabbed her eyes.

'No,' she began. 'A letter … Papa's family … three aunts, two uncles and all of my cousins … all ended up in Auschwitz. All dead now.'

I thought about how hard it was for us when one person died in our family and that person died of what Granny called 'natural causes'. But here was my friend, getting news about several deaths. And all in one letter.

'Were they…?' I couldn't bring myself to say the word.

She bit her lip and nodded.

'Oh no! That's awful, Karla.' I rubbed her arm. The horror of what she had just found out – what words could I use to comfort her?

Karla said something in her own language.

'Sorry, Nancy,' she said then. 'I am so shocked; I don't know what I am saying.'

If this was the news about her relations, what was she going to hear about her mother and sister? As if she could read my mind, she said, 'Still no word about Mama and Vera. What hope have I now after hearing such news?' She wiped her eyes again with her hankie.

'Are you all right, Karla?' someone called out from across the street. It was Mrs Hanlon. She was walking alongside another woman. They both had the same pixie-like faces – it had to be her sister who was pushing a cart full of old clothes. The two women crossed the road.

'Ah, the poor young one,' said the sister.

'She's had some very bad news,' I said.

'Sorry to hear that, love. What bad—' began the sister.

'Leave them alone, Dolores,' said Mrs Hanlon. It could be something private. If you need me, girls, I'll be home after six.'

'Thank you,' said Karla in between sobs. She stood, resting her head against the wall. Her nose was red and her eyes were bloodshot, but she was starting to breathe normally again. 'Home. I long to go home, but what's home if there's nobody left?'

'Don't give up hope. You might get some good news yet.'

'How do you say it in Ireland … "fingers crossed"? I will try my best to stay hopeful, but it is very difficult. You asked me about Levi? I am meeting him this evening.'

'Does he know anything about his parents?'

'Like me, he awaits news. The poor boy frets but does not like to talk about it. With Levi it's work, work, work all the time.'

'In college or in Eppenstal's?'

'Both. That way he keeps the worries out of his head. What about you, Nancy? Please tell me you have some good news. You have heard from your Aunt Gretta, perhaps?'

Given all that she had to cope with, I wasn't going to mention the letter, but when she asked, I felt I had to tell her.

'That account of the Pig Farmer and your grandmother … does it not seem strange to you that two good friends would disagree because one didn't follow the other's advice just one time? I wonder if there is something more that we are not being told about?'

'Didn't think of it like that, but sadly it looks like Aunt Gretta isn't going to change her mind about us.'

'What a cold woman,' said Karla quietly. 'Throwing away a chance to love and be loved.'

★ ★ ★

Once dinner was over that evening, and the tidy-up done, I ran down the steps into Gloucester Place. I skipped past the girls with the skipping-ropes, playing 'Up the Ladders, down the Spouts', and ran through a gang of boys playing 'Relieve-ee-o'. The smell of dead animals in Thorne's Hide and Skin Factory made me hold my breath, as always. When I arrived at Willet's Place down in the Diamond, Maggie was putting out dinner for the twins.

'You've news, love?' she said when she saw me. I told her about Fr Comiskey's talk with Aunt Gretta. She shook her head.

'Isn't that pure unnatural?' said Maggie. 'She has no children herself. Wouldn't you think she'd be delighted to have yiz?'

'Yeah,' said Lilly. 'You could have looked after her in her old age. Now she's depending on some auld one. God knows, she could be gone before her.'

'What'll I tell the others?' I asked.

'The truth,' said Maggie, mashing up some potato with a fork on Breda's plate. 'It's a hard thing to do, but it's the brave thing to do. And you … you're one of the bravest girls I know, Nancy Kidd.'

Lilly put two mugs of milk on the table and swung around to put her arm around my waist.

'The Kidds won't be leaving Summerhill now. I for one am glad. But sorry for the reason that's making you stay.'

I smiled, but inside I was screaming.

★ ★ ★

'And that's why she said we can't come over,' I concluded. I was sitting at the kitchen table on Ma's old chair. I held Aunt Gretta's letter in my hand. There was silence for a few seconds.

'Can't come,' repeated Tom. 'Is this some sort of joke?'

'Tom Kidd, would I joke about something like this?' I said.

'I can't believe that Aunt Gretta could be so cruel,' said Kate. 'I always thought she was some kind of fairy godmother.'

'I still don't understand why she's cross with *us*. It's not fair!' Tom shouted the last three words.

'Don't take it out on Nancy,' said Kate. 'She's only telling us what was in the letter.'

Patrick's lower lip went down. 'I was looking forward to playing on the swings and slides in the playground near her house,' he said. 'And I was hoping Aunt Gretta would buy me a dog.'

'Now listen, everyone. We're all upset. We're annoyed with Ma and Granny for keeping the secret, with Aunt Gretta for being cross with them and taking it out on us, and with the Pig Farmer for writing to Aunt Gretta. But it's the Pig Farmer that we have to be careful about now. We can't afford to cross her.'

'Ever since I picked up the missal that time in the church, she says "hello" to me,' said Kate.

'I still wouldn't trust her.' It was hard to imagine the Pig Farmer saying 'hello' to any of us after years of ignoring us.

'And I still don't like the smell of her,' said Patrick.

'None of us does, but she'll be watching us, especially me. A word from her to the Cruelty Men could mean that we're split up and sent away to Goldenbridge or Artane.'

'Do those places have swings and slides?' asked Patrick.

'No,' I said.

'Do they have dogs?' he asked.

'Most certainly not. They're awful places. That's why we need to make sure that we stay together here.'

'Mrs McGee asked me yesterday were we still going to Leeds,' said Patrick.

'Let me handle Mrs McGee,' I replied. 'Are you all right, Kate?'

She stood in front of a wedding photo of Honora and Joe Murphy that hung on the wall. Our grandparents … so we always believed.

'What about the other grandmother, the one in the laundry? I wonder what her name was and where did she come from?'

'I had a look through Ma's things to see if I could find her birth cert, but there was no sign of it.'

'What about asking at the laundry?'

'I think the nuns keep all of those details private,' I said. 'We'll probably never know.'

Chapter Eighteen

I may have got a job as a runner in Mandel's, but I was still expected to dress smartly. And now it was even more important to turn myself out well. As we weren't going to Leeds, I'd be after a permanent job. Ma's two good skirts still hung on hooks in her bedroom. The house was quiet on Tuesday evening, so I picked out the prettier one with tiny roses on a faded green background, and ripped the stitches of the seams to cut it down to my own size. Once that was done, the skirt had to be stitched back up on the machine.

My fingers felt the metal handle of the wooden case under Ma's bed. Granny's pride and joy, a Wertheim sewing machine, was inside it. I pulled it out and carried it to the kitchen table. This was the first time to see it there since Ma had used it for Mrs Deegan's blouse.

Kate breezed in from the library, a couple of books under her arm. She stopped when she saw the sewing machine.

'Fixing a skirt for work,' I said, threading the needle with a green thread from the new spool I had put in. I worked it up and down on a seam, but the stitches came out all knotted. I tried to adjust the bobbin, but it made no difference.

Kate looked up.

'Are you stuck?'

'Afraid I am. The tension is wrong, no matter what I do. Who will I get to help? I needn't ask Mrs McGee. I heard her say once she can only sew by hand.'

'What about Mrs Perrin?' asked Kate.

'Could you go and ask her?' I said. My legs were aching from all the messages I had run at work today.

'Please?' I added.

She made a face and threw her eyes up to heaven.

'All right. I will.'

She put the library books on the top shelf of the dresser. I undid the stitching on the seam and had it ready to go again. A minute later, Kate came back.

'She said to tell you she's sorry, but she can't help you.'

'Maggie doesn't know either, so no point going there. Can you think of anyone else?'

'Ma used to go to Mrs White.'

'Mrs White in number 28? She moved out to Cabra last month.'

I thought for a few minutes. 'You know who might be able to help me?' I said, folding up the skirt and putting the case back on the sewing machine. 'Karla. She knows all about sewing machines. I'll ask her if she can come around on Saturday.'

'So, we're finally going to meet the famous Karla,' said Kate. 'Make sure it's the afternoon so I won't be at work.'

* * *

The following Saturday morning, after I had washed the clothes, Patrick and I spun into a frenzy of cleaning. He swept the floor and dusted the mantelpiece and the sideboard. Granny's big china jug that Ma had brought her from Leeds had become grimy grey of late but was now back to sparkling white. I cleaned the grate, scrubbed the floors and washed the windows. I covered the table with Granny's linen tablecloth – the one with the harps and the lacy edges – and put the sewing machine in its case on top.

Kate came home from work.

'The place never looked as clean,' she said, sliding her finger along a shelf of the dresser. There was a loud knock on the door.

I opened up and in walked Karla, with a bag under her arm and a smart straw hat on her head.

'You must be Kate,' said Karla, walking forward with her hand out.

Kate shook her hand. I could see her admiring Karla's hat. Karla took a book out of her bag.

'I have read this,' she said, handing the book to Kate. 'Nancy told me you're a great reader. I thought you might like it.'

It was a worn copy of *Anne of Green Gables.*

'Thanks. I haven't read it, but I've heard it's a great story.'

Karla took off her jacket and threw it at the back of the chair. Before sitting down, she whipped off her hat and placed it on the table beside the sewing machine.

Sconsie started singing 'Kevin Barry' out in the hallway.

'I like your hat,' said Kate.

'My friend Levi suggested that this little feather would make it look very smart.' She touched the feather lightly. 'By the way, do you remember a man waved to you on the street that time – outside the convent in Sean MacDermott Street?'

I muttered 'yes' under my breath.

'He's out there on the stairs now.'

I felt my cheeks burn.

'I said I didn't know him that day—' I was trying to find the right words.

'Sconsie?' said Kate. 'That's because Nancy'd prefer if he didn't knock about in our hall.' Kate was looking me straight in the eye to see what I would say.

'I've nothing against him—' I began, but I couldn't think how to finish. Anything I said would make me look like I was trying to cover over what I'd done that day. I patted the top of the sewing machine case. 'Here's the machine causing problems,' I said, hoping that the subject of Sconsie was closed. I unfastened the locks and took the cover off.

'A Wertheim sewing machine! Your grandmother had good taste, Nancy. Now let's see if we can improve the tension.'

She adjusted the bobbin as I had done and tried some stitching on a piece of fabric I gave her.

'No good. So, let's adjust the tension nut here.' She tightened a little nut at the side of the machine and tried sewing again.

'Ah, that's better.'

No sooner had she said these words than somebody burst in the hall door and started running up the stairs. The boots on the bare wood sounded like a stampede of cattle from Smithfield Market had made its way into the building.

Karla jumped up and ran around to my side of the table.

'What's that?' She grabbed my arm tightly.

'Open up, Mrs Boland!' shouted a voice upstairs.

'Who is that?' asked Karla. She was trembling, still holding my arm. She whispered something in her own language.

'It's the guards. Ray must have escaped again.' I stood up and tried to get her to sit in my place, but she stood frozen to the spot. We could hear a door being opened, followed by men's voices asking where Ray was. The whole building could hear them.

'I don't know anything about him,' shouted Mrs Boland.

'Where is he?' a guard demanded loudly.

'I don't know, Mister.' It was a little girl's voice now and she was crying. This was followed by a big crash. Karla leaned against the wall and covered her ears. It sounded like saucepans were being thrown around upstairs.

'That's all the tin mugs and plates,' said Kate. 'After the first time all her delph was smashed, Mrs Boland went and bought tin ones instead.'

'Mr Boland did something very bad?' asked Karla.

'*Mr Boland*?' repeated Kate. 'Mr Boland died two years ago. It's Ray they're after.'

'What did he do?' asked Karla.

'He missed too many days at school,' I said.

'You're joking?' She looked at me to see if I was. 'You're not! A boy has been sent to prison for missing school?'

'Not prison but that place I was telling you about – Artane.'

'Where Charlie is?' asked Karla.

'That's the place.' For a moment, Charlie's handsome face with his cap turned sideways flashed into my mind.

'Leave my childer alone,' shouted Mrs Boland. 'None of them know where Ray is, no more than myself. This is the last place he'd come to hide, and well you know it. Leave us alone.'

'This is his third time to run away,' said Kate.

'That's his mother shouting upstairs?' asked Karla.

'It is. Since her husband died, the poor woman's been trying to make ends meet.' Karla looked confused so I explained, 'That means scraping enough money together to pay for everything. You know why Ray was missing from school? He had to look after the little ones in the family when his mother was at work. He was given "a warning" for that. But over the next few months he missed a lot of school. He often had no clothes to wear because his ma had to pawn them.'

'Six years they gave him,' added Kate. 'He was only ten.'

There was more banging. The guards had slammed the door closed and were running down the stairs. We could hear Sconsie curse at them as they passed him on the stairwell.

'For not going to school … I can hardly believe it. Could nobody explain why he was missing?' asked Karla.

It was one of those 'Karla questions' that I didn't know how to answer. I shrugged my shoulders.

'That's the law,' said Kate. 'And we've to be very careful here. The Cruelty Men are *always* on the lookout for children they feel are not being looked after properly. Seeing Ma and Da are both dead and Nancy is still so young, they'd think nothing of puttin' us into those children's homes.'

Then we had to explain to Karla who the Cruelty Men were.

'My goodness, it sounds more like the "Society for Cruelty *to* Children", if you ask me.'

She sat down, turning her attention to the sewing machine, and started working on a seam.

'I hope the poor boy is safe, wherever he is.'

Chapter Nineteen

As soon as Karla left, I put the finished skirt across the back of a chair and climbed the stairs to Mrs Boland's room. Mrs Perrin and Mrs McGee were sitting with her at the table. All the plates and mugs were tidied up and the two little girls were lying on their palliasses with a blanket over them.

'Do you need anything?' I asked.

'If you can spare a sup of milk, I'd take it, Nancy,' said Mrs Boland. I was turning around to go and get it when she added: 'And could you let Maggie know that Ray's done a runner.'

'I'll get Kate to bring you up the milk and I'll pop over to Maggie's,' I said.

It was still bright as I made my way down the twenty-seven steps. A group of girls were chanting 'Old Granny Grey' at the 'granny' – a little girl in a dirty blue dress and bare feet. I hurried through them before she took off chasing after them. In Willet's Place, I opened the door into Maggie's house. Mona was reading a newspaper at the kitchen table. Imelda held a black kitten, while Breda and Mary each held a piece of string, making them sway slowly back and forth, teasing the little ball of fluff.

'Careful, he'll scratch you!' said Lilly. 'Hi, Nancy. That's our new kitten.'

'Yours? I thought I heard Maggie say she'd never get a cat.'

'She used to say that, but she's fed up with the mice keeping us awake. Last Saturday night, the four of us lay on our palliasses on the floor in that corner, and not for love nor money could we close our eyes with the little terrors. Ma had a word with Brian Dardis outside the church in Gardiner Street and this little lad arrived by teatime.'

'His name's Jerry,' shouted one of the twins. 'We wanted to call him Tom but Ma wouldn't let us because that's your brother's name.'

'Is your ma in?'

'No, she's had to go over to Auntie Bridie.'

'Everything all right?' asked Mona, folding up the newspaper.

'Ray Boland has done a runner again from Artane. Mrs Boland asked me to come over to tell Maggie.'

'Were the guards around?' asked Mona.

'They were. The neighbours are over with her now, looking after her.'

'Wouldn't you think that fella Ray would have more sense? They'll give him an awful time when they catch him,' said Mona.

'Maybe he won't be caught this time,' I suggested.

'It'll be a miracle if he's not,' said Mona.

'I wonder if Charlie knew he was goin' to do it?' I said.

'Don't know, but you can be sure I'll ask him tomorrow.' Lilly petted Jerry. 'I'm headin' out to visit him on my own. Ma's friend Chrissie is home from London and they want to meet up.'

'I've offered to look after Imelda and the twins,' said Mona. 'Otherwise, I'd love to visit Charlie. I miss him and his cheeky sales pitch outside the laundry these evenings.'

'We miss him around here – not just for the money, but for the laughs and slagging we'd be goin' on with,' said Lilly.

'And what about Jerry?' asked Mary, scratching the little kitten under its chin. 'Charlie never even got to see him.'

'He'll see him soon enough. He'll be let home in a couple of weeks on a home visit.'

The talk of Charlie made me think of his handsome face, the gap in his teeth and how much I missed him. All thoughts of not having the nerve to visit him in Artane were pushed aside.

'Would you like some company?' I asked.

The kitten freed himself from Mary's clutches and darted across the kitchen.

'Jerry!' shouted Mary.

'Something tells me that my nephew would be very happy to see *you,*' said Mona. 'What do you think, Lilly? Would he like extra *company* tomorrow?

Lilly laughed and looked at me. 'Company? Of course he would, and so would I! What time will I call around for you?'

★ ★ ★

Maggie insisted on writing a note to say that I was Charlie's cousin, in case there was any fuss made of a girl visiting who wasn't a sister. So, here we were on the 42A bus, heading out the Malahide Road. Lilly held the letter in one hand and a couple of liquorice laces for Charlie in the other. I remembered he liked bullseyes; in my pocket, I had a penny's worth rolled up tight in a newspaper cone.

Most of the passengers on the bus got out at the stop nearest the school. There was a crowd of Artane lads waiting inside the gate, some of them as young-looking as Patrick. They were all squashed behind a couple of older boys who were standing straight, and carefully watching visitors through the gates. Some boys were going out with their families. The gatekeepers called out names when they spotted someone's ma or da or brothers or sisters.

On seeing Lilly, a thin-faced boy with a shaven head waved at us. The grin on his face broadened when he saw me behind her. One of the gatekeepers shouted 'Charlie Weaver'. That was our cue to go in. The bruising around his eye had turned a horrible colour of yellow. The first thing I missed was his cap, but I knew that if I were to get through this visit, all thoughts of caps had to be switched off.

Lilly had the letter ready, but the big lad said, 'Go ahead, Miss', and we jostled through all the boys towards Charlie.

'I'm honoured with a visit from Miss Kidd of Summerhill,' he said, tapping my arm. His voice was husky like he had a sore throat.

'Now, now, she's our cousin, according to this letter from Ma,' said Lilly, holding the envelope up.

'The lads call this "the crying mile",' said Charlie, nodding towards the avenue going up to the school. He led us through droves of boys, some with their mas and das, others strolling in groups together. Minutes earlier, we had stepped off a city bus, but now it felt like we were in the middle of the country, with a stone quarry on our left and cows grazing in the field on our right.

'I keep gettin' the smell of cabbage,' said Lilly.

'That's from me,' said Charlie. 'I'm working in the kitchen, and as cabbage was on the menu today – as it is most days – I'm reeking from it.' He coughed, trying to clear his throat.

'Your voice sounds funny,' said Lilly. 'Have you a sore throat?'

'Yeah – but that's the least of my worries,' said Charlie. 'Did yiz hear about Ray Boland?'

'The police were in with his ma last night,' I said. 'They gave the place the usual going over.'

'First I heard of it was when Brother Staunton lined us up outside before bedtime and started shouting at us 'til he was hoarse,' said Charlie. 'He's the brother in charge.'

'Ray didn't tell you he was going to take off, then?' asked Lilly.

'Not a word. I've hardly been talkin' to him since I came here, to tell you the truth. Was talkin' to his ma once when she came out to visit.'

'No word about him this morning?' asked Lilly.

'None. They must be still looking for him.'

'How have *you* been, Charlie?' said Lilly, stopping to face him.

Charlie shook his head. He checked to see who was around before answering in a whisper, 'Couldn't begin to tell you. I used to think we got a bad time in the red-brick slaughter-house, but that's only a babby house in comparison to this hellhole.'

We walked on, nobody talking. Lilly broke the silence.

'Why are you walkin' funny?'

'Sore legs. This morning I was carrying a huge saucepan full of boiled cabbage across the kitchen and spilt some water from it. The Brother in charge of the kitchen – Briscoe – took his leather strap and beat the backs of my legs.'

'He beat you?' said Lilly, stopping to look at the back of his legs. He was wearing short tweed trousers and thick socks pulled up to his knees.

'Don't, Lilly,' said Charlie, and he kept walking. 'I'll get in worse trouble for saying anything. What did you bring me to eat?'

'A couple of liquorice laces,' said Lilly, taking them out. 'Mona dropped them in for you.'

'And I've brought a penny's worth of bullseyes,' I added, holding them out.

'Great. Let's eat them first,' he said, taking the bullseyes and popping one into his mouth. He handed them back to me to take one. I passed them on to Lilly.

'No difference in the food?' Lilly asked, with a bullseye inside one cheek.

'What do *you* think? I'd kill for a bit of decent grub *and* to get away from the rats! Think we have rats in Summerhill and the Diamond? Pah! They're only sugar mice when you see the vermin this place is crawlin' with. Us kitcheners have to keep after them non-stop.'

'Tom was asking for you,' I said, trying to brighten up the chat a bit.

'Glad to hear it. I hope he's watchin' out for the badge man? You don't want him ending up in a kip like—'

'How'ya, Charlo,' said a boy passing us by with his mother and grinning back at Charlie.

'How'ya, Toff,' answered Charlie. The boy and his mother went ahead of us.

'He loves toffees, so that's how he got that nickname. And he's not the only one of his family stuck in a place like this – his sister's in Goldenbridge.'

'Speaking of Goldenbridge, Nancy knows about Aunt Lizzie,' said Lilly.

Charlie looked at me and nodded. 'From what I hear,' he said in a low voice, 'it hasn't changed much.'

We passed a man with a boy each side of him, both dressed in Artane uniforms.

'See those workshops over there?' Charlie said, pointing to some buildings over on our left. 'That's where the traders work. Toff works in the tailors' workshop.'

We were in front of the main building now, a big grey structure that reminded me of a hospital. There seemed to be hundreds of windows and I imagined a Christian Brother standing at each of them, staring out at us. We passed a statue of Jesus, his arms stretched out wide as if to welcome us. But our three heads turned towards the door as a grey-haired Christian Brother came bounding out in our direction.

'Here's Briscoe,' Charlie said under his breath.

'These are your visitors, Weaver?' he asked, keeping his eyes on Charlie.

'Yes, Brother, my sister and cousin,' said Charlie.

Lilly produced the envelope and, without a word, the Brother took it from her, tore it open, and read the letter.

'Why don't you bring your sister and your ... *cousin* ... over to the chapel to say a few prayers?' he said, scowling, as he walked off, putting the letter into the pocket of his soutane.

'My only prayer is to get out of this place,' said Charlie under his breath. When we turned the corner, he checked again, to see who was within earshot among the many visitors strolling around the grounds.

'He's bad enough, but there's another one – Brother Heaney – I'd be warier of. He saw me talking to another lad during Mass my second morning here and waited for me outside.'

'For what?' I asked.

'To punch me in the face. Told me that's what I got for showing disrespect at Mass. Sure, look at the right shiner he gave me.'

'Why didn't you tell that to Mrs Boland?' asked Lilly.

'Because she'd tell Ma and hasn't the poor woman enough on her plate? And to be honest, if Ma came out here and said anything – and you can be sure she would – it'd make things worse for me.'

We were going into the chapel and a little boy came out the door.

'Frank, do you want a bullseye?' called Charlie. 'Now, you're only to take one!'

He held the paper cone out and Frank snatched a sweet and ran away.

'Poor little chap arrived last week. He was livin' with his ma some place down the country and when she died, there was nobody to take him, so he ended up here. I was polishin' the floor in the front hall when they brought him in.'

'What about his da?' I asked.

'Don't know about him. Frank's the same age as your Patrick. Lilly, remember what Mona used to tell us about Aunt Lizzie in Goldenbridge and the wet sheets? That poor little fella had to stand in his nightshirt at the wall in the dormitory for two hours last night because he wet the bed the night before.'

I imagined what it would be like for Patrick to come to a place like this the week after Ma died, and I shuddered. We sat down on the last seat in the chapel. It was dark and cool. The smell of incense competed with Charlie's cabbage-smelling clothes. An old Christian Brother with a head of thick white hair was kneeling on a kneeler in front of a statue of Our Lady, whispering his prayers. Charlie put his fingers up to his lips to tell us not to talk. We sat quietly for a few minutes, sucking our bullseyes. Then Charlie moved his hand over and took mine and squeezed it. I let his hand rest on mine. All he was going through because of two words spoken by me: *Charlie Weaver*. It wasn't until we heard the door opening that he let go of my hand and we stood up to leave. Once outside, the bright sunshine hurt our eyes.

We continued on the avenue that now took us through a farmyard. A big heap of cow dung was piled in one corner.

'I keep thinking I'm in the country,' I said.

'More like a *different* country,' said Charlie. 'This place is run like it was a country on its own. Everything that's needed is made here, by us, of course. See this jacket?' he said, pulling at his sleeve. 'Made over in the workshops. Even the stuff it's made of is made here. I hate it. It's hard and scratchy.'

'I thought it was a school. They always call it an "industrial school",' I said.

'More like a "Get Everything They Can Out of You School",' muttered Charlie.

'What's that place there?' I asked, pointing to a two-storey building on the right.

'That's where they send you if you're sick. It's called the infirmary. I was sent over there when I got the black eye. I was sittin' in the hall for two hours before a nurse came to check me.'

'What did she say when she saw it?'

'Nothing. She dressed it but asked no questions. Afraid of the answers, you can be sure,' he said, half laughing. But his face became serious almost straight away. He put his head down and spoke in a whisper.

'The two hours I sat there, I was thinkin' the whole time.'

'About what?' asked Lilly.

'About the best way to get out of this kip. I'm not stayin'.'

'What do you mean you're not stayin'?'

'I'm plannin' on doin' a runner.'

Lilly and I stopped. She spoke first.

'I thought you had more sense than Ray Boland. Remember the last time he was caught?'

'I'm smarter than Ray,' said Charlie. 'He thought he could take off on his own. You're wasting your time at that. If you want to do it right, you need to get help from the outside.'

'Who would you get?' asked Lilly.

'I'm thinking of Da's old friend.'

'Hairy Bacon?'

'The very man.'

Hairy Bacon, a docker, lived in Corporation Buildings.

'Not sure if he'd be up for it,' said Lilly.

'I think he would,' said Charlie, looking around again. He lowered his voice even further. 'Didn't he spend the best part of four years down in Letterfrack when he was a young fella? Oh God, when I think of the stories he told me, and I thought he was makin' half of them up.'

'In fairness, he was a good friend of Da's,' said Lilly.

'Will you go and see him? Tell him I have to get out of here and I'll need help to do it.'

We stopped talking for a minute while a gang of boys passed us by.

'If I was able to escape from this place, I wouldn't hang around Dublin to be caught again. I'd be over to England straight away! Over to work on the buildings.'

It was the first time he sounded like the old Charlie.

'I'll go to see him, but don't get your hopes up,' said Lilly.

Charlie put his arm around her.

'Ah, poor Sis. Worrying that I'm going to be let down.' We had arrived at the other gate and a couple of 'gatekeepers' were on duty. 'Thanks for the bullseyes, Nancy,' he said loudly, but he leaned over and whispered to Lilly.

'Please go and see him.'

Then he took my hand and shook it. *If only I had more time in the chapel to hold that hand*, I thought.

'Thank you for visiting me, dear cousin.' He winked and walked away. There were no goodbyes. The boys at the gate let us out and we didn't look back.

Chapter Twenty

On Saturday afternoon, there was a queue of people waiting to use the tap in the back yard. I stood with the bucket, chatting to Mrs McGee. Once the person ahead of her was gone, Mrs McGee's large plaid-shawled back leaned forward as she placed her bucket under the tap.

'Wouldn't you be killed going in and out for buckets of water – dragging them up and down the stairs?' She turned on the tap. When the bucket was full, she lifted it up. 'Sh! Who's that talking?' she whispered.

The conversation was coming from the far side of the high wall at the end of the yard – where the Pig Farmer kept her pigs. The talk, as well as the smell, drifted towards us.

'What's that, Mrs Kelly? She tore strips off someone?' The Pig Farmer asked the question in her nasal voice.

'Off your woman living in the basement. She sells flowers in O'Connell Street. Her sister Dolores is a tugger. Maggie came across her in the Daisy Market on Saturday.'

'The Hanlon woman?' asked the Pig Farmer.

'That's her. Someone saw her going into Reilly's shop the morning Charlie's cap was found and, of course, that "someone" went and told Maggie.'

'And?' asked the Pig Farmer.

'To tell you the truth, when Maggie tore into her, she gave back as good as she got. Told her in no uncertain terms that she'd never snitch to the guards like that.'

'Well, I don't know where that rumour started, but I can tell you for a fact, it wasn't her,' said the Pig Farmer.

'Wait a minute … you know who it is?' said Mrs Kelly in awe.

'I do,' said the Pig Farmer, clearly enjoying the importance this gave her. I went to put on the tap to fill my bucket, but Mrs McGee held my hand to stop me and shook her head.

'Who was it?' asked Mrs Kelly.

'I was wonderin' that myself,' Mrs McGee whispered to me. 'Here's our chance to find out. Don't turn on the tap for a minute.'

I stood with my bucket and my hand on the tap, trying to think of some noise I could make that would stop the talk on the far side of the wall. But my body felt as if it had been struck by some power that wouldn't let it move.

'Oh, I wouldn't be going around announcing that in public, Mrs Kelly. But I'll tell you what I *will* do. As soon as I'm finished here, I'm going around to Buckingham Street. *I'll* tell Maggie Weaver the name of the real culprit, and all I'm sayin' is, she'll be surprised when she hears it.'

'Buckingham Street? Sure, the Weavers live in the Diamond,' said Mrs Kelly.

'The Diamond?' repeated the Pig Farmer.

'Yes, in Willet's Place. They're living there this ten year. You're thinking of where Maggie grew up. The Molloys – *they* lived in Buckingham Street.'

Mrs McGee poked me and pointed at the wall.

'Mrs Perrin said the Pig Farmer's been actin' very strange of late,' she whispered. 'She missed Mass on Sunday and arrived on Monday at eleven o'clock, wondering where everyone was.'

On the far side of the wall, the Pig Farmer was talking again.

'Oh, that's right. The years go by so fast. It's hard to keep track of where people are living. I'll head over there now and talk to her directly.'

Mrs McGee leaned over and whispered, 'You can find out later from Lilly so.' Some of the water from her bucket splashed onto her skirt as she turned to go. 'And let me know, like a good girl.'

The water couldn't fill the bucket fast enough. I had to get to Lilly's before the Pig Farmer. I dragged the bucket into the kitchen. Kate was boiling the kettle on the fire.

'Where's Patrick?' I asked.

'Brendan called for him.'

'When he comes back, will you ask him to get some fancy bread? I'm leaving the money and the pillowcase on the table.'

'Where are you going?'

'I've to go over to Lilly's,' I said. 'I won't be long.'

★ ★ ★

As I dashed up the street towards the archway into the Diamond, my head swam with all the different ways of telling Lilly that it was me …

'Boo!'

I was so caught up with the conversation I was having in my head, I almost tripped on the footpath from the shock of this shout. Jemmy and Mickser jumped out from under the archway and started laughing.

'Look at her face!' said Mickser. 'You'd swear she saw a ghost.'

'Not now,' I said, pushing past them, but I hadn't gone three steps before Mickser passed me out and stood in front of me.

'Any loose change in your pocket?' he said.

'None,' I said, trying to get by him. Jemmy's voice came behind me.

'No money? So, you're no better off than us.'

'It'd only take you a minute to go back and get some,' said Mickser. He stood on the step below the one I was on, daring me to go forward. I looked behind him to see was there anyone I could call. It was strange to see the place so quiet.

'Let me by,' I said.

'Let her go,' said Jemmy. 'She's no use if she's no money on her.'

But Mickser didn't look like he was going anywhere in a hurry. He seemed pleased that I was afraid and I could sense he enjoyed the power he felt it gave him over me. He stood with his hands in his pockets.

'I'll let her go when I'm good and ready,' he said, keeping his eyes on me. 'There's the matter of—'

Just at that moment, a boy's voice bellowed from the archway behind:

'Quick, lads, there's been an accident.'

'Where?' Mickser leaned to the side to look past me.

'Outside Hogan's.' This was a bar and grocery at the corner of Summerhill and Gardiner Street. Such news was more than Mickser and Jemmy could resist. Mickser pushed past me, tearing back up the steps after Jemmy. My legs felt so weak, I sat down on the steps for a minute. Two little boys wandered over from Murphy's Cottages. They found a couple of old sticks at the bottom of the steps and started scratching out lines in the dirt.

'What's your name?' one of them asked me.

'Nancy,' I said.

'Fancy Nancy!' said the other boy and they both ran off laughing. I watched them go and as soon as my legs felt steady, I took off towards Willet's Place. Lilly would hear all about the story of Charlie's cap from *me*; it wasn't going to be easy – but letting her find out from the Pig Farmer was unthinkable.

As I slowed down to go into Weavers', a boy's voice shouted my name behind me.

'Nancy! Nancy Kidd!'

It was Jemmy.

'For God's sake, can't you leave me alone?' I said.

'No, wait. There's been an accident.'

'So I heard,' I said.

'It's your Patrick that's been hurt.'

'What? Stop it! That's not funny!'

'I'm not joking. Himself and Brendan were scuttin' on the back of a truck and they fell off.'

'Patrick … scutting?' I said. Little Patrick, my nervous little brother, jumping onto the back of a truck. 'Are you sure it's Patrick?'

'Dead sure.'

'He's not…?' I said.

'No,' said Jemmy quickly, 'but he's badly hurt. Brendan isn't as bad. They've brought them both off to the Mater.'

My little brother! I had to turn around.

'Thanks, Jemmy.'

★ ★ ★

The cold stone steps curved up towards the main door of the Mater Hospital. It brought back memories of the Richmond and Ma lying on the slab in the mortuary, her pale lips and her hair brushed back off her thin face. And now, Patrick. Kate was close behind me. She had insisted on grabbing Bob, Patrick's old teddy, to bring with us. We pressed the bell, framed in a circle of bright brass.

A porter popped his head out. His long chin pointed at us over a white starched collar. When he saw we were children, it seemed like he looked behind us, to see if anyone else was coming up the steps to make it worth his while to have opened the door. He barely opened his lips as he asked us our names.

'You're here to see…?' he said.

'Patrick Kidd. He was in an accident.'

The face softened when he heard the word 'accident'.

'Come in, come in, good childer,' he said kindly.

He showed us into a room off the hall, as he disappeared through a pair of heavy wooden doors, with patterned glass full of squares and diamonds. The strong smell of furniture wax reminded me of the convent in Sean MacDermott Street. The porter was hardly gone out the door when an old nun popped her head in. Eyes made bigger by her thick glasses, she asked us our names and the name of the person we had come to visit. I was wary of saying too much. All I could think of was the story of Lizzie in Goldenbridge, but this nun didn't seem like the ones Mona had told me about. Her voice was soft and her face looked kind.

'So, you're here to visit your brother Patrick – the wee lad that was brought in there a half an hour ago? What about your parents?'

'Both dead,' I said.

'And who's minding ye?' she asked.

'I am,' I said.

'God love you, aren't you a great girl? I can tell you Patrick's under the care of Mr Archer – an excellent surgeon. I'm heading down to the chapel now and I'll light a candle for the poor wee lad. Ah, here's Nurse Gillick.'

A pale woman with a white veil nodded when she heard her name.

'Thank you, Sister Olivia,' she said as the nun made her way back out to the hall. 'Patrick's still in surgery,' she said, when we gave our names again. 'Why don't you come and sit in the corridor? Someone will come to talk to you when he's brought out.'

She led us into the inside hall. It was very grand, with a big stone staircase in the middle. Jesus stared down at us from a huge picture hanging on the landing where the staircase split in two. He had a red shawl draped over one shoulder and was pointing to his sacred heart. But the nurse didn't go up the stairs. We followed her through double doors into a corridor. It had big windows – bigger than the ones in the Tin Church. She pointed to the nearest one and we perched on the shiny wooden sill beneath it. Kate was crying quietly and hugging poor old raggedy Bob.

Countless nurses, doctors, nuns, visitors and patients had passed through the corridor by the time Nurse Gillick came looking for us.

'They had to stitch a bad cut on his head and they're worried about the bang he gave himself. He also broke his right leg,' said Nurse Gillick.

'Can we see him?'

'Not this evening, he's—'

'Will he be all right?' I couldn't bear standing there a moment longer without finding out.

'We can't say yet, but we're keeping a close eye on him. I see you've brought in a teddy from home. I'll take that and tuck it in with him, later.'

We made our way among the other visitors through the corridor with high ceilings like a chapel, back to the big front door with the brass handle and the fancy brass fittings. From there we ran down the steps into Eccles Street and hardly spoke a word on our way back to Summerhill.

Chapter Twenty-One

On Sunday it was decided that I would go to the hospital in the morning, and Kate and Tom would go in the afternoon. Sister Olivia was walking the corridor, saying her rosary. She clutched the bead she was on and broke away from her prayers.

'You're here to see wee Patrick? Wait here until I talk to the nurses.' She went into the nearest ward, but the door didn't close fully behind her.

'What's the story on Patrick Kidd?' I could hear her say.

'Not good,' a nurse answered. 'He's in intensive care. Took some sort of a seizure during the night and had to be moved.'

'His sister's in to visit him.'

'She won't be able to see him this morning. We had to tell the last visitor the same last night.'

'Who was that?'

'A man from the NSPCC.'

'Oh?' said the nun.

'A man called Sharpe. Asking about the family, he was. Parents both dead, neighbours keeping an eye on them, but when something like this happens, they're very quick to put it down to the lack of proper guardianship.'

My heart almost stopped when I heard the last bit. Why

were they snooping around now? I had thought that by giving them Charlie's name, there would be no more worrying or watching for the Cruelty Men. Somebody noticed the door was open and shut it. I couldn't hear what was said after that. Sister Olivia arrived out shortly after and toddled over to me.

'Och, you could be waiting a long time to see your brother this morning, Nancy. He had a bit of a setback and isn't allowed visitors.'

'A bit of a setback? What does that mean?'

She sat down on the window sill beside me and patted my arm.

'Injuries to the head sometimes cause seizures and that happened to wee Patrick during the night. He's being very carefully watched now by the doctor and the nurses, and that's why they don't allow anyone else in, even family.'

'When can I come back?'

She looked at her watch.

'I'd say come back after tea – maybe around half-six. Please God, we'll have good news for you then.'

I got up, my stomach churning. *Please God, we'll have good news?*

'Nancy!' Sister Olivia called after me, but I couldn't turn around. I had to get out of that hospital. Outside, I sat on the stone steps that swept up to the main door, trying to convince my legs they had to move and bring me home.

Mrs McGee was in with Tom and Kate when I got there.

'Patrick isn't as well as we hoped,' I told them. 'I wasn't allowed in to see him.'

'Will we be able to see him this afternoon?' asked Kate.

'No, but if you like, you can come back with me this evening.'

'I made a big pot of stew for the dinner,' said Mrs McGee. 'We've all eaten so you're welcome to what's left.'

'Thanks, Mrs McGee,' said Kate. 'No cooking for me today.'

'Will you come upstairs with me and bring it back, Nancy?'

I followed her out and she spoke to me quietly in the hall.

'One of the Cruelty Men was around yesterday evening,' she said. 'He was up with poor Mrs Boland. They've caught Ray.'

'Is he back in Artane?'

'No, they've transferred him to Letterfrack – that place over in the wilds of Connemara. His poor mother's in bits. She'll never be able to afford to go over to see him there. But listen, the Cruelty Man came down to me after.'

'And?'

'Said his name was Sharpe. Was asking about yourself and how you were managing. I told him that you were doin' a great job and Mrs Perrin and meself were keepin' an eye on yiz, but I didn't like the way he was going on. He was asking about what happened to Patrick and sayin' that there should be an adult livin' with yiz, "a guardian" is what he said.'

She climbed the stairs and I followed.

'He was asking about us in the hospital, too,' I said.

'I told him I'd vouch for you, Nancy, but you know what they can be like. They make up their mind and it's very hard to turn it around.'

Inside in Mrs McGee's kitchen, the stew was still on the table, surrounded by bowls and spoons that had to be washed. She handed me the saucepan to take with me. It was still warm.

'It was such a shame your Aunt Gretta let yiz down the way she did,' she said. 'Wouldn't she have been the ideal guardian to row in and help you? But never mind. We'll do our best, love, to make sure you stay with us.'

'Thanks for the stew!' I called as one of the little girls opened the door for me on my way out.

The three of us sat at the table and hardly a word was spoken. Kate had her pale, worried face on, and Tom kept scowling. All you could hear was the sound of the stew being slurped up from the spoons.

A loud knock was followed by Sconsie shouting: 'A message there now from the parochial house. You're to go to the Mater straight away.'

'Thanks, Sconsie,' I shouted back, jumping up. Tom's face was the colour of chalk. 'Is it like Ma all over again?' he said, half talking to himself.

'You're not to say that, Tom Kidd!' said Kate. 'You're not to say that.'

***

Fr Comiskey was waiting in the corridor for us.

'I've given Patrick the last rites,' he said. 'They sent for me as soon as they started getting worried about him.'

Last rites. The last sacrament you're given before you die. The last two words we wanted to hear.

'He's unconscious and it's not looking good, I'm afraid. We're waiting on Mr Archer to come and check him. He should be here any minute. You'll have to wait here.'

A nurse came out of another room and walked towards Fr Comiskey.

'Mr Young is looking for you, Father.'

'Sorry, I have to go. I'll enquire again about Patrick before I leave.' He hurried down the corridor, passing Sister Olivia on his way.

'Ah, you poor wee creatures. I've just been in to see Patrick.' Sister Olivia pressed the cross that she wore on a chain. 'It feels as if God is calling him home,' she added, like a quiet prayer in a chapel.

How could she be so calm? Tears of rage stung my eyes.

'We don't want him to be called home,' said Tom. 'Tell God to leave him where he is.'

'It's not up to us to question His will,' said Sister Olivia, still speaking gently.

Our little world was being shattered, but life around us seemed to be going on as normal. Heels clicked on polished wooden floors, patients were discussed in whispers, notes and charts were checked. There were even people brushing the window sills with feather dusters. None of us spoke. What was there to say?

A man wearing a white coat paraded down the corridor, followed by four men who were learning to be doctors, and a couple of nurses. He checked the notes he had on his clipboard.

'In here next.'

'Yes, Mr Archer,' said one of the nurses.

We might as well have been a couple of statues on the corridor, the way they all passed us by. The door closed behind them and we were left waiting. I closed my eyes and thought about Patrick. The way he loved to play with his little pretend cars, buzzing all around the kitchen. The way he said 'grace' with a lisp when he was saying his prayers. I remembered the day he stole a piece of cake that Ma had put away in the big tin and walked through the kitchen holding it in his hand. He kept his eyes closed, thinking that by doing that none of us could see him.

It seemed like hours before the door of the ward opened. Kate, Tom and I stood up. But the doctor, the medical students and the nurses once again passed us by and continued without as much as a glance at us. This time I wasn't going to let them go, though, and I ran down the corridor after them.

'Excuse me. Could you please tell me how my little brother is?' I called.

Mr Archer stopped and the students and the two nurses nearly crashed into him. They looked around to see who could have had the cheek to address the great Mr Archer, to ask a question and expect to be answered.

'One of the nurses back in the ward is going to talk to you,' said the nurse closest to the doctor. She spoke to me like a teacher telling a bold child to go back to her seat in school.

'No, it's all right, Nurse McKee,' said Mr Archer, moving forward. 'Your brother's condition caused a panic during the night, but having examined him, I am optimistic that he's going to pull through, Miss eh …' – he looked at his notes – '… Kidd. You can go in and see him now.'

By this time, Tom and Kate were beside me. Sister Olivia had come back out from the other ward.

'Oh, praise be to God,' said the kindly nun, on hearing these words. 'Isn't it—'

We didn't wait for the sentence to finish. All we wanted to do was see our little brother. We hurried back down the corridor and into the ward. Patrick was in a bed with metal bars on each side. A nurse was fixing his sheets. His eyes were flickering open. I held his hand, half crying with relief.

Tom took Bob up from the little bedside locker and tucked him in beside Patrick.

'Look at the special little visitor that came to see you,' he whispered.

Patrick didn't say anything but there was a faint smile on his lips.

'It looks like God has changed His mind,' Sister Olivia said as she shuffled over towards us, smiling.

Chapter Twenty-Two

'What a weekend you had! Poor little Patrick.'

On Monday morning, Karla sat beside me in the kitchen at work, keeping her voice low. 'Where were you when it happened?'

'On my way over to Lilly – to tell her something important, but I never got to.'

'Something important?'

'About Charlie. I'll tell you later.' Keeping the story of Charlie's cap to myself was beginning to feel like a wound that had festered. If I didn't share it with at least one other person, it would never heal.

'And I have news too,' said Karla. 'We will talk later. Yes?'

Once one o'clock had struck, Karla and I walked towards the quays. The story about what had happened in Reilly's shop that morning came pouring out. I told her about taking the cap and how the policeman had forced me to give Charlie's name. I told her about hearing the Pig Farmer and Mrs Kelly talking the day of Patrick's accident.

'I'm the one who destroyed their family,' I said. Tears stung my eyes.

'She is an old friend. She will understand you had no choice.'

'I don't think Lilly will see it like that,' I said sadly. 'And she must know by now. The Pig Farmer said she was on her way over to tell Maggie.' We stopped to let a delivery boy cross the footpath into a yard. 'Lilly will probably be over tomorrow to tear me to shreds – that means to be very angry with me,' I explained quickly when I saw a look of confusion on Karla's face.

'Even if she knows that you were going over to tell her?'

'She'll be raging I haven't told her before now,' I said.

We walked along in silence.

'You told me Charlie was thinking of running away from Artane,' said Karla.

'Yes, but that might have been all talk. He thinks an old friend of his da working on the docks will help him, but I don't know. Helping the likes of Charlie is breaking the law so people are slow to do it … I wish I could help him.'

'Maybe you could?' suggested Karla.

'What? You're joking, aren't you?'

'I am not. The worst thing that happened was that Charlie ended up in Artane. If you want to make things better, why not help him to get out of there?'

'It's not that simple.'

A plan to help Charlie escape? I may as well head out to sea in a little rowing boat during a storm. After Patrick's accident, I needed some time in calm waters before thinking about anything like this. A pair of seagulls landed beside an apple core on the pavement and squabbled loudly over it.

'And you've got news, too, Karla?' I asked, suddenly remembering.

'A letter came from Miriam. Mama and Vera were still alive in Terezín on 25 April.'

'That's great! How did she find out?'

'Bette, her cousin, called to tell her. She knew Mama in college. Bette arrived in Terezín on that date, after the Germans forced her to walk all the way from Buchenwald in Germany.'

That sounded like a long way, but I didn't ask Karla about it. We were talking about her mother and sister. At last, she had heard something about them.

'You must be so happy to get some news.'

'Of course, but after that date – nothing! They are no longer in Terezín and nobody knows where they are. Happily, their names are not on the list of the dead. Do you know what I think? They are safe somewhere else because somebody helped them. That tells me I should do the same for Charlie.'

I reminded her about what had happened to Ray Boland, but she shrugged her shoulders and tapped her forehead.

'We are two very smart girls, are we not? We will make a good plan. What a pity there was nobody to help Ray, but Charlie has people willing to help *him*. Having people makes the difference.'

'You know, Charlie said the same thing to Lilly and me, the day we visited him in Artane. He said if you want to do it right, you need to get help from the outside.'

'You see! He is a smart boy, too. You know who might also help us?'

'Who?'

'Levi.'

'I'm not sure if it'd be a good idea to get him involved,' I said.

'Would you mind if I talked to him about it?' asked Karla.

Karla knew Levi, but I didn't. How could I know that he could be trusted?

'Please don't be worried about trusting him,' said Karla, reading my mind. 'I would trust Levi with my life.'

'All right. But I'm still not sure if it's a good idea myself.'

'Why not leave it for the moment and let me talk about it with Levi? I will be seeing him this evening. I have no doubt he would want to help us if I asked. You've got to think of your little brother.'

The way Karla said 'if I asked' made me think that Levi would do this out of love for her, but the mention of my little brother turned my thoughts to the Cruelty Men.

'My little brother is one of the reasons why it's hard for me to think of helpin' Charlie now.'

'It is all too much for your brain?'

'No, because the Cruelty Men are watchin' us again.'

I told her about what I had heard in the hospital and about the visit to Mrs McGee.

'My poor Nancy,' she said. 'After all that has happened, you think these Cruelty Men might still come after you and put you away into those terrible places?'

I nodded.

'They are upset because a proper guardian is not living with you?'

'That's what I heard the nurse say – and Mrs McGee. And now it's really important to have someone when Patrick comes out of hospital.'

'Is there somebody you can ask?'

'You know the story of Aunt Gretta. She was the one person we felt we could always go to. Other than that, Ma was an only child, so we've no aunts or uncles in Ireland. Da's ma lives in Leeds and we barely have any contact with her.'

Karla opened her purse, took out a little mirror and checked her hair.

'What about me?'

'You?' I said.

She kept her eyes on the mirror.

'Couldn't I be your guardian?' she asked. She dropped the mirror into her bag. 'They're looking for someone to be there when Patrick comes out. I could stay with you.' Karla as our guardian! I never would have thought of asking her, but could she be the answer to our prayer?

'Don't forget we've no electricity or running water.' I was also going to remind her about the privy outside with the rats running riot, not to mention the bugs and mice indoors, but I didn't.

'I can tolerate that,' she said.

'You know, neither Kate nor I could bring ourselves to sleep in Ma's room. That could be your room.'

'First, you must talk to your sister and brothers about it,' said Karla. 'If they are happy to have me, I could come next weekend?'

★ ★ ★

'She'd be paying rent,' I said. 'Not as much as she did in her last place, but it'd be a nice bit of money coming in for us.'

'But she's going to be sleeping in Ma's room,' said Tom. 'Don't feel happy about that.'

'If I've to choose between having Karla move into Ma's room and going to Goldenbridge, I'd choose Karla any day,' said Kate.

'You and Kate know her, but I've never met her,' said Tom.

'She told me that I can tell you her story,' I said. 'That way you'd have a better idea of her.'

And I told them.

'All her aunts and uncles to die like that,' said Kate. 'And her cousins! I'm going to light a candle in the church and pray she'll hear from her ma and sister soon.'

'Has Lilly ever met her?' asked Tom.

I had pushed all thoughts of Lilly aside because of Patrick's accident. What must Lilly be thinking now that she knew about what I had done?

'Once,' I said.

'By the way … Mrs McGee told me to tell you that Lilly called around yesterday and left a message to say that she'll be around Tuesday evening,' said Tom.

Tomorrow was Tuesday. So, I would finally have to face Lilly over what I'd done.

'Thanks, but let's get back to what we were talking about. Are we all happy for Karla to move in?'

'I'm happy,' said Kate.

'Yes,' said Tom, shrugging his shoulders.

⋆ ⋆ ⋆

I spoke to Karla the next morning at work.

'Kate and Tom are willing to welcome me? I feel so happy to hear that. What about Patrick?'

'Why don't you come to the hospital this evening and meet him yourself?'

'What a good idea! You once said that his favourite sweets are bonbons. I will call to the shop on the way and buy some.'

'He'd love that.'

'If Patrick is agreeable to my moving in, I'll talk to the Rosenbergs tonight. Since the last baby has been born, there is very little room. They will be happy to have more space.'

'Will it make a difference that we're … not Jewish?' I asked.

'Yes, it will,' she said. 'But leave that with me. And I told you that I could move in at the weekend, but it will be Sunday rather than Saturday. It would be unthinkable for me to move on the Sabbath.'

'Your Sabbath is on Saturday?' I asked.

'That's right. I may not be religious, but the Rosenbergs are.'

We walked on quietly and I thought how odd it must be to have what we thought of as our Sunday on Saturday.

'I've other news,' I said. 'Lilly is calling over this evening.'

'The Pig Farmer got over to her the day of Patrick's accident? She knows the truth now?'

'She must know it by now,' I said.

'Then why not tell her about our idea of helping Charlie to escape?'

'It's only an idea at the moment. I'd rather wait until we have a plan before I say anything.'

'I was talking to Levi last night.'

'Yes?'

'I told you before that he works part-time for Eppenstal's. He told me that they sometimes make deliveries to Artane.'

'Deliveries?'

'Yes, like bales of cotton. If we could get Charlie into the delivery van and brought to the docks to get on a boat for

England, there would be a good chance that the escape would work.'

'If Levi is caught, he could go to jail,' I said. 'I've got enough people in trouble as it is.'

'If it's well planned, he thinks it could work and so do I. We need to find out about Charlie's docker friend first. His help is all important.'

I paused.

'You're sure Levi's up for it?'

'You mean that he is prepared to do it?'

'Exactly. I can't go telling Lilly about it only to find out that Levi was only thinking about it.'

'He said that he would be prepared to help. I know him and he means it. "How many times did people stand by and do nothing at home?" we asked ourselves. Tell Lilly we are both definitely "up for it".'

'If that's the case, can you find out when Levi's next delivery to Artane is?'

'I will meet him today during our break and I will ask him then,' she said.

* * *

That evening, Karla and I stood on Foley Street after work, a red rose pinned onto the lapel of her jacket.

'I didn't notice that earlier,' I said.

'Levi picked it in the grounds of Trinity College.' Karla filled me in on what she and Levi had discussed.

'The next delivery is on Thursday, 14 June.'

'That's the day of the elections,' I said.

'Yes, Levi said the same. People will be going around thinking "Which person would I like to be the next president?"'

'Or "What person do I want on Dublin Corporation?" That could work well for us.'

'He said we would have to make sure to bring Charlie some clothes to change into. That is one of the ways people know Artane boys straight away. He also said that you should dress as a boy to go with him as he could not think of bringing any of the regular boys with him.'

'Why does he need someone with him?'

'Eppenstal's always have what they call a "van boy" with the driver, so we must do the same so nobody will be ...'

'Suspicious?' I offered.

'That's right. The more it looks the same as other deliveries, the better.'

She went through the plan Levi had discussed with her. It ended up with Charlie going to the docker's house.

'What if Hairy Bacon doesn't agree to help?' I said.

'Hairy Bacon? Who on earth is that?'

'That's the docker. His surname's "Bacon" and that's why his friends gave him the nickname "Hairy".'

'You will have to explain what hairy bacon is some other time, but our plan depends on getting help from him.'

'I've a feeling he'll help all right. He was in one of those places himself. He knows what it's like for Charlie.'

Karla paused when the church bells chimed.

'I have to go now, but I will see you later at the hospital.'

Chapter Twenty-Three

'Hello, Nancy. Had to come to see the patient,' said Mrs Delap. She and Brendan had arrived in a corridor in the Mater Hospital when visiting time began. I walked with them down to the Children's Ward. A nurse sat at a desk in the middle and behind her were three cots. On each side of the room was a row of beds. Patrick was in the third on the left, sitting up in bed, drinking a glass of milk.

'How are you, love?' She patted Patrick's arm.

'Sore and thirsty,' said Patrick, pushing his teddy under the covers.

'But you're going to be all right. It'll take a bit of time. We've come from the Garda Station. Went there this morning to make a statement.'

'About the accident?' I asked.

'You can be sure it was about the accident. These two boys were driven to get up on that lorry by a couple of gurriers in their class. Teasing them unmercifully about their fathers bein' in the British Army.'

'Those lads were at it again?' I asked Patrick.

'They said we were both cowards because our dads had joined the Brits,' said Patrick. This was followed by a sob.

'And if we wanted to show that we were brave Irish boys, we'd scut the same as them,' said Brendan.

'Well, they haven't heard the last of it from me,' said Mrs Delap, a fiery look in her eyes. 'Isn't it only the mercy of God that spared Patrick from following your poor mother, and my own lad to walk away with only a few scratches?'

As soon as we were on our own, I gave Patrick a hug.

'Don't listen to those boys about Da, Patrick,' I told him. 'And you don't have to show them or anyone that you're brave. Now, I've got some news for you.' I told him about Karla.

'Is she like a new ma?' he asked when he heard she was moving into Ma's room.

'More like another big sister than a ma,' I said.

'Does she like dogs?'

'Why don't you ask her yourself?' Karla had just walked into the ward.

'Hello, Patrick.'

'Hello, Karla. Do you like dogs?'

'I don't like them,' she said. 'I *love* them. We had the sweetest little dog at home called Lenni.'

Patrick asked all about Lenni and then moved on to the second subject dearest to his heart.

'What about cars?' he asked.

'I cannot drive yet, but buying a car is one of the first things

I want to do when I have enough money. By the way, how do you like bonbons?'

By the time Karla left the hospital, she had the youngest Kidd's approval to move in.

★ ★ ★

I asked Kate and Tom to be out later that evening. I told them that I needed to talk to Lilly on my own. Her familiar footsteps echoed in the hall. I heard her stop to talk to Sconsie. She said something and he laughed. The door opened and she came in. I poked at the fire, waiting for the shouting to begin, but all she did was plop down in Ma's chair.

'How's Patrick?'

'He's … getting better,' I said, still expecting the row to start.

'I came over on Sunday when I heard, but you were all gone to the hospital. Ma and I couldn't believe it when we heard what happened. Such a quiet little fella and to think of him—'

'I know. We couldn't imagine him at it either,' I said. I didn't feel like explaining about the lads teasing Patrick. All I could think was: *When is she going to say what she really came over for?*

'I don't know what the world is comin' to,' said Lilly, making herself more comfortable in the chair. 'The Pig Farmer came over to see Ma on Saturday.'

'The Pig Farmer?' I said. Here it was coming.

'That was a shock for sure, seeing the likes of *her* standin' at the door.'

'What did she want?' I asked, dreading the answer. I sat down on a kitchen chair.

'Now that's a question I would find hard to answer,' said Lilly. 'She started mumblin' something about her husband, Martin – like he was still alive. And, would you believe it, she asked if we'd seen Honora Murphy. She said she had a bone to pick with her.'

'Granny?'

'Yeah. When Ma tried to explain that she was dead, the Pig Farmer changed the subject and asked Ma about the next sodality meeting.'

'That was odd,' I agreed, wondering if it could be possible that Lilly still didn't know about me and the cap and Charlie.

'Then she said that she had come over to tell Ma somethin', but couldn't remember what it was. She said she'd go home and come back again and that way it'd come back to her.'

'And did she?'

'She went home all right, but she never came back. We're still none the wiser.'

She didn't know, but I felt I'd have to tell her now.

'I've something to tell you, Lilly, and it's very hard for me,' I started.

'What? God – is it something you didn't tell me about Patrick?'

'No, it's about your Charlie.'

'Yeah?' When Lilly heard 'Charlie', she grinned and raised her eyebrows. I knew that look. She was expecting me to tell her how I felt about her brother.

'The day that the cap was left in the shop, the Pig Farmer and a guard in plainclothes were there and so was I. I spotted the cap and tried to hide it up my cardigan to give back to Charlie, but I was caught.'

'What?'

Lilly sat up straight, her mouth slightly open.

'Then the guard wouldn't let me go unless I told him the truth about who owned the cap. I swear, Lilly, I wasn't going to tell him, but he told me that if I didn't, our family would be split up and sent to Artane and Goldenbridge.'

Lilly stood up.

'Don't tell me it was you!'

'The Pig Farmer even said she had the Cruelty Men watching us. Said I was a child minding other children.'

'*You* gave Charlie's name?'

'I didn't have any choice.'

'Didn't have any choice, oh that's rich. Couldn't you have said you didn't know whose it was?'

'I told them I thought it was Tom's first, but they didn't believe me.'

'Could you not have made somethin' up?'

'I tried to, but I was so scared, I couldn't think of anything.'

'Oh, you've plenty of ideas when it comes to savin' your own skin, but when it comes to your best friend, that's another story.'

I stood up.

'I thought I was being a good friend by trying to take the cap in the first place. I'm sorry that I couldn't think of something smart like you can, but I was afraid.'

'*You* were afraid and look where that landed us? My ma half out of her wits with worry that the family's goin' to be split up! My brother's in Artane! All thanks to you.'

'At least you have your ma,' I shouted.

'And what would *your* ma have made of this? Her daughter turnin' out to be a snitch?'

The door opened. Mrs McGee put her head around it.

'Girls, girls, will yiz pipe down? I'm trying to get the baby to sleep. Can the pair of yiz take your argument outside, please?'

The two of us standing each side of the fireplace looked at her, red-faced.

'Sorry, Mrs McGee,' I said. She gave a stern look at Lilly and shut the door.

I moved over to the table and Lilly followed. We sat down at opposite ends, Lilly glaring at the red and yellow flowers on the oilcloth.

'Look, Lilly, there's something I can do to make up for what I did.'

'Make up? I doubt it.'

'Listen and give me a chance.'

'Off you go. I'm all ears,' she said in that cutting way herself and Maggie always had when they were cross.

I started to tell her about Karla, Levi and the plan.

'Stop right there!' She stood up and banged the table with her fist. 'You told a "stranger" about us. Someone I hardly know?'

'Will you just listen and give me a chance?'

'Why should I? How do I know I can trust you and Carol or whatever her name is? And she's gone and told another fella called Levi? Why don't you print your fancy plan on the front page of the *Herald* while you're at it?'

'Look, I was forced to tell on Charlie. Now I'm trying to make up for it. Will you sit down and listen!'

She dropped onto the chair, eyes fixed on the oilcloth.

'Go on then.'

I started talking. When I paused, she fired a few questions at me. I answered all of them. She asked some more. Clearly, she was starting to be impressed by the plan.

'What about Hairy Bacon?' I asked. 'Have you been over to him yet?'

'I went over one evening, not long after we were out in Artane. He asked me if Charlie was coming home on a Sunday visit and I told him we were expecting him this coming Sunday.'

'And what did he say?'

'He wants to talk to Charlie in person.'

'What about your ma?'

'As far as Ma is concerned, he's coming over to see Charlie to advise him how best to handle things in Artane. She doesn't know anything else.'

'Do you think Charlie will like our plan?'

She stood up. A sulky look returned to her face as she shrugged her shoulders.

'He mightn't want to trust the very person who put him in there.'

I stood up.

'That's true, but he might be willing to let bygones be bygones when he finds out the risks that person is taking to get him out.'

Lilly's two hands were on the table and she had that mad stare in her eyes. But it didn't last.

'Let me think—'

'It's not just me. Levi is taking a huge risk getting involved too.' Lilly's face began to soften. 'What about if you went out some evening this week and talked to Charlie? Is he allowed visitors on a weekday?'

'He is if I make up some sob story for the Brothers, but …

things are very tight at home. To tell you the truth, we couldn't spare the price of a bus fare out to Artane.'

'Come on, Lilly,' I said, going to the bowl on the dresser. 'We're not going to let a bus fare get in the way of a great plan.' I took out a couple of coins and handed them to her.

'It'll be a while before I can pay you back,' said Lilly, taking the money and putting it into her pocket.

'Who said anything about paying me back?'

'Tomorrow's Wednesday. I'll head out in the evening to see Charlie.'

'Great. And come over here to us on Thursday and tell us how you got on.'

And for the first time since she'd arrived, she smiled.

Chapter Twenty-Four

'You shouted at one another? Of course, you did. As we say in Prague, neither of you "walk around hot porridge". You both said what was on your mind.'

I had a picture of Lilly and myself standing knee-deep in hot porridge, shouting at each other.

'When we both cooled down, I told her about the plan.'

'And?'

'She liked it, but she wants to talk to Charlie about it, so she's going out to Artane this evening to see him.'

'What about that man – Hairy Bacon – will he help, do you think?'

'We think he will. Charlie is coming home on Sunday and Hairy is coming over to visit him.'

'They let the boys out sometimes? Don't they run away then?'

'No. They allow Sunday visits because the families know how hard it would be for them *and* the boys if they don't come back. The guards would be out searching for them straight away.'

'Maybe *we* could meet Charlie and Hairy on Sunday?' said Karla. 'When is Lilly meeting you again?'

'She's coming over tomorrow evening,' I said. 'I'll get the latest from her about Charlie then.'

★ ★ ★

On Thursday evening, as I was getting coddle ready for the dinner, the door gently opened.

'Are you on your own?' came a voice behind me. Lilly walked in, took her hat off and sat down at the table.

I put the coddle on the fire.

'I am, indeed. The others are visiting Patrick.'

She sat down.

'Got to see Charlie. He wasn't happy when he heard about what happened with the cap. Of course, I had to tell him all about that first—'

'And the plan?'

'He's all for it! He said if you help him to get out of that kip, he doesn't care what you did.'

'And you're sure nobody heard you out there?'

'Do you think I came down in the last shower? I told the Brother in charge that Ma had sent me to tell Charlie our auntie was very sick. Then I asked him if we could both go down and light a candle for her in the chapel. That's what we did and got to talk on the way.'

'And he's still coming home on Sunday?'

'He is. He wants to meet you and Levi. Could you all meet over here? Charlie says there'd be no chance of discussin' anything in our house.'

'What'll you tell your ma?'

'I told her that Hairy Bacon wants to talk to Charlie to advise him how to survive in Artane and that it might be too upsettin' for Imelda and the twins to hear what he had to say.'

'Good thinking. As it turns out, Levi had planned on being here on Sunday anyway. He's comin' over with Karla.'

'Is he her boyfriend?' asked Lilly.

'As far as I know, he is, but with working and studying and all, he doesn't have much time to spend with her at the moment. I didn't get to tell you the other night that Karla's moving in and Levi's going to help her.'

'Movin' in?'

'The Cruelty Men were snooping around, since Patrick's accident. Said to Mrs McGee that there was a lack of "proper guardianship" in our house. They were poking their noses in at the hospital too.'

A rap at the door stopped us. Before I could stand up, Mona marched in.

'All right, I want to know what's goin' on. Maggie just told me some cock-and-bull story about Charlie meetin' Hairy here on Sunday. You may have taken her in, but not me!'

Lilly and I looked at each other.

'Charlie wants to get out of Artane,' said Lilly quietly.

'And?'

'We're plannin' to help him.'

'Are yiz out of your minds?' She swiped the hat off her head and put it on the table in front of her. 'I had the pair of yiz down as sensible girls.'

'I think we'll have to go back and tell her everything,' said Lilly, looking over at me.

And we did. I started with the morning in Reilly's and what had happened over Charlie's cap. Unlike Lilly, Mona listened calmly and said she could see how I was forced to give Charlie's name. When we described the plan for his escape, she kept interrupting me with questions like 'But what if he doesn't get into the van?' or 'What if you're stopped on the Malahide Road and searched?' but we were able to answer all of her questions.

'I'm just worried that if it doesn't work out, Charlie will be sent off to somewhere like Letterfrack or Daingean,' she said. 'Look what happened to our Lizzie all those years ago. Look at what happened to Ray Boland.'

There was a tone in her voice, though, that told me she was coming around.

'I've a couple of suggestions,' she said after a few minutes. 'Bring Charlie's boots in the van with you. As well as the clothes, those old hobnailed boots the lads wear in Artane are always a giveaway. Also, I think myself and Lilly could be useful at Amiens Street Station. If there are too many guards around, we could stage a fight and cause a distraction.'

'The boots are a good idea,' I said. 'Let's talk to the others about the "fight".'

'One last thing,' said Mona. 'Lilly, do you realise that Nancy and all her family could end up in industrial schools if she's caught?'

Lilly looked at me and for the first time ever I saw her stuck for words.

'Don't worry,' I said. 'We've thought of all of that. We're going to try our best to make sure *not* to get caught.' Lilly and Mona left together and I could hear their chatter through the open window as they went down the street.

★ ★ ★

On Sunday, the church bell chimed two o'clock. I checked Ma's bedroom one last time. Crocheted cover, clean pillow-cases, the pot or 'the goes under' under the bed. The basin in the washstand was clean. Kate bought a couple of purple daisy-like flowers from Mrs Hanlon at a very good price and placed them in a jam jar on the washstand. A note beside it read 'Welcome Karla to Summerhill from Kate'. Over the top of the bed, a large rectangle of wallpaper was lighter than the rest of the wall that had been darkened by smoke over the years. We had discussed whether or not to leave Granny's picture of the Holy Family hanging there, but as Karla was coming to sleep in the room and we needed the money, Kate hocked it down at the pawnshop.

Less than ten minutes later, Karla and Levi stood at the door. Levi had two bulging carpet bags. Karla had a bag made out of cotton that was also full, as well as her handbag.

'And as I was her beast of burden this far,' said Levi, 'you might as well tell me where to put these bags before I shake hands with you.' He smiled and his dark skin made his teeth look very white. His black hair was slicked back and if you told me he had walked off the set of a Hollywood movie, I would have believed you. I brought the pair of them into Ma's room, and Levi put the bags on the bed.

'Oh, this is delightful, Nancy,' said Karla. 'I have not had my own room since I left Prague.' She stopped and read the note beside the flowers. I was surprised to see tears in her eyes. 'And flowers 'specially for me! What a lovely thought from Kate.'

'I know it's still kind of part of the rest of the room because the wall only goes up part of the way, but that's so that you'll have a bit of light in here.'

Levi shook hands with me and we went back into the kitchen.

'And if you put the kettle on to boil, I've brought some tea with me that I bought with my coupons on Friday,' said Karla.

'And I have brought some sugar,' said Levi.

I hung the kettle on to boil and Levi and Karla took off their jackets and sat down at the table.

'Nice skirt,' said Levi to me. I was wearing one of Ma's that I had cut down. I couldn't help but blush. Karla had never mentioned how handsome Levi was. 'Hairy and Charlie are coming soon?'

'They'll be here any minute,' I said.

By the time I had scalded the teapot and thrown in the tea-leaves, Hairy and Charlie had joined us. This was our first time to meet since he found out I had told on him. I couldn't look at him straight in the eye.

'Charlie and Hairy, this is Karla and Levi.' Hands were shaken all round. Charlie took off his serge tweed jacket and Hairy whipped off his cap and set it on the mantelpiece. He rubbed the back of his shiny bald head and pulled out a chair. Once he was sitting at the table, he started telling us stories about his time in Letterfrack and being put out to the fields to pick stones. He showed us a scar on his hand from a cut that he got during his time there. Although his stories told of a horrible time, they helped Charlie and me through this awkward meeting. When I plucked up the courage to look over at him, I could see that he was watching me. We finished our tea and got down to business.

'Well, ladies and gentlemen,' said Hairy. 'I believe the order of the day is to discuss the exit of one Charles Weaver from an institution known as St Joseph's Industrial School, Artane.'

Charlie cleared his throat.

'And I would like to inform the present company that Mr Henry Bacon, also known as Mr Hairy Bacon, is a member of the Irish Seamen and Port Workers' Union and is known to have a way with words.'

'Thank you, Charles, but let's get to the matter in hand. Levi, you're making a delivery to the school on Thursday?'

'Yes. We have an order for the infirmary and the workshop.'

'What time?' asked Charlie.

'We usually do the run in the morning – no set time.'

'Could you leave it until about half-twelve? I'm on kitchen duty at that time. This week, I'm haulin' the slops out to the pigs, so I could slip down from the farm easily enough to the infirmary.'

'We will leave the back doors of the van slightly open. If for any reason you cannot be there, we will stop at the workshops next,' said Levi.

'That's a harder place not to be seen,' said Charlie. 'But once you're there before all the boys come out for dinner, it could be done.'

'There will be bales of cotton in the back, as well as piles of flour bags,' said Levi.

'Don't forget that I'm going to be dressed as one of the shop boys sitting up front,' I said. 'Levi said he always has one of the young lads from a Jewish family, so I'm going to be "Isaac" on the day.'

'What did you tell Eppenstal's about not bringing one of their regular boys?' asked Hairy.

'I told them I was approached by a Jewish boy who was looking for a job as a van boy and that I could try him out for them. They are so busy at the moment, they said to go ahead. When I go back next time, I will tell them he turned out to be unsuitable.'

'Now to return to the plan: in the back of the van there will be a bag of clothes for you to change into,' said Karla to Charlie.

'And your own boots,' I added.

'When you have changed, throw your Artane uniform and boots into that bag,' said Levi. 'I will stop the van on the Malahide Road at a bus stop. Nancy will get out. She will make sure to take the bag with her, and she will go back into town on a bus.'

'Will I stay in the back?' asked Charlie.

'No,' I said. 'This is where you hop in beside Levi. Anyone looking at you sees the driver and van boy that went into Artane School earlier.'

'What happens next?' asked Charlie.

'I will have to drop a parcel off at Amiens Street Station,' said Levi. 'You can get out there.'

'Mona and Lilly said they could stand by at the station and

start a row if the guards need to be distracted.'

'That's an excellent idea,' said Hairy.

'So, I get out of the van?' said Charlie.

'And walk down to my gaff in Corporation Buildings,' said Hairy. 'My missus'll be there, expecting you. I'll be home around six o'clock and we'll get you down the quays to the boat for Liverpool. It doesn't leave until nine. There'll be—'

Loud pig-like snorts were coming from the hall. It wasn't a pig but sounded like one of the children trying to make pig grunts. This was followed by a rap on the door. Hairy signalled to Charlie to step into Ma's room. Karla was closest to the door and opened it.

The Pig Farmer stood, one hand on her walking stick, the other holding the corners of a black shawl together.

'Good afternoon,' said Karla. 'Can I help you?'

The Pig Farmer stared at her.

'Is Mr Sharpe here yet?'

'Mr Sharpe?' Karla looked over at me. I shook my head.

'You must have the wrong address,' she told the Pig Farmer.

'Wrong address? Of course, I haven't the wrong address. He must be here. He always keeps his appointments. He told me that he'd be here on the twelfth at four o'clock. I've just heard the clock chime four.'

'It is four o'clock, but today is the tenth,' said Karla.

The Pig Farmer stared at Karla.

'That couldn't be right,' she said. 'I've made two cups of cocoa next door. One for myself and one for Mr … Mr …'

'Sharpe?' said Karla.

'That's right. I thought he was coming today, but now that I think of it, he wouldn't work on a Sunday. He keeps the Sabbath, does Mr Sharpe. Not like some people I know.' She gave her cane a rap on the floor and looked over the table. 'Ned Bacon! I hope you're not about to play a game of cards on the Lord's Day.'

'You're mixing me up with my da,' said Hairy Bacon. 'We're only having a friendly chat, Mrs Knaggs.'

'And what about you, Jenny?' she said to me.

'There is no Jenny here, and no cards, so if you'll excuse us, please?' said Karla.

The Pig Farmer paused as if making up her mind whether to leave or continue talking. 'I'll leave yiz, so.'

Karla closed the door. 'Who on earth was that?'

'That's our famous neighbour, the Pig Farmer,' I said. 'And the Mr Sharpe she was talking about is one of the Cruelty Men. He must be coming on Tuesday.'

'It's not like her to be mixing up those dates and me with my da,' said Hairy. 'He was friendly with her husband.'

'She called me Jenny, whoever that is,' I said. 'You can come out, Charlie.'

Charlie came out of Ma's room. His grin made me feel

everything was all right between us; he knew I was doing my best to make up for what I'd done. He knew the risk Levi and I were taking. His face became serious as he sat down again at the table. *This is the last time to see him before the day of the escape*, I thought. *And after that? God knows how long it will be.*

'There's one more thing we didn't think about when we were talkin' about the escape,' he said. 'I'll have to get some money for England. I know I'm going to get work and all that, but I can't go over with empty pockets!'

'If things weren't so stretched with me—' started Hairy.

'I might be able to get a loan for you,' said Karla.

'Ma and I couldn't pay back a loan at the moment,' said Lilly.

'I'll be makin' good money at the buildings. I'll pay it back myself,' said Charlie.

'Jacob will only deal with people who are living in Ireland, so could you send the money back to Lilly and let her look after it? Write down the amount you want and give it to me,' said Karla.

I tore a page out of an old copybook of mine and, after a short discussion, Charlie wrote the amount that he needed. The piece of paper was handed to Karla.

There was another rap at the door. Sconsie stood there, smiling.

'How did you like my pig squealing? I was trying to warn yiz that your wan was heading for your door. She had a face on her of someone that was up to no good.'

Chapter Twenty-Five

On Tuesday afternoon at four o'clock, there was a terrible commotion in the hall. All the doors opened and all the upstairs neighbours came out to lean over the banisters to see what was going on. A man in a gabardine coat and a woman in a tweed suit were trying to get past Sconsie in the hall. They had only managed to get through the front door.

'State your business,' Sconsie kept shouting. 'You'll not get admission to this house until you state your business.'

'Stand aside, man,' said the man in the gabardine coat.

'Our business here is no concern of yours,' said the woman. She spoke as if she were holding her breath, afraid she was going to catch something from Sconsie.

Mr Evans from upstairs put his hand on Sconsie's shoulder.

'You're only aggravating the situation, Sconsie,' he said. 'Let them by to do their business.'

I closed the door. In a matter of seconds, they would be knocking on it.

Karla winked at us. When the knock came, she took her time opening it.

'Good afternoon,' said Karla.

'Good afternoon, Miss—' said the man.

'Popper,' said Karla.

'I am Mr Sharpe and this is Miss Spatt. We're from the National Society for the Prevention of Cruelty to Children.'

'Yes?' said Karla.

'We are concerned about the welfare of the Kidd family and are here to investigate their circumstances.'

'I see,' said Karla. 'May I see your identification, please?'

'I beg your pardon?' said Mr Sharpe.

'In my country, officials are required to present identification when they are entering a private citizen's dwelling. I am using the right word – "official" – yes?'

'I can assure you, Miss Popper, this is highly irregular. In this country, we are trusted by the people. They believe we are who we say we are.'

Karla still held the door.

'*They* may believe you, but *I* have never seen you before, so I would like to see your identification, please.'

He made a clicking sound in annoyance and put his hand into his trouser pocket to pull out his wallet. As he fished out his card, Miss Spatt opened her briefcase and did the same. Karla checked them and handed them back.

'Thank you, both. You are now welcome to enter.'

Miss Spatt whispered something to Mr Sharpe. After they had both marched in, she placed the briefcase on the kitchen table, which was covered by Granny's good linen tablecloth, and turned to Karla. 'Now that we have shown you *our* identification, we'd like to see *yours*, Miss Popper.'

'Of course,' said Karla. She pulled out her handbag from the drawer of the dresser, opened it and took out her passport. Miss Spatt checked it and handed it to Mr Sharpe, who looked at it quickly and handed it back.

Kate was sitting beside the fire, a library book on her lap. Tom was sweeping the ashes on the hearth with a little hand brush and shovel, and I sat at the kitchen table with my sewing.

'May I present to you the Kidd family?' said Karla. 'This is Nancy, the oldest, then Kate and, as you can see, Tom is there at the grate. As no doubt you are aware, their youngest brother, Patrick, is at present a patient in the Mater Hospital.'

'And who are you to this family?' asked Mr Sharpe.

'I am a cousin of their late father's. If you are investigating this family, you already know that Thomas Kidd was from Leeds. His mother, Ellen Cohen that was, and my mother, Rebecca Cohen, were sisters.'

But not of each other, I added in my head. My Leeds granny was born Ellen Cohen all right, but she came from a little farm outside Westport in Co. Mayo, where she lived until she emigrated to Leeds.

'Would you like some tea?' I asked.

'Yes, please,' said Miss Spatt.

I put on the kettle to boil and Kate put out the good cups and saucers, our precious sugar and Granny's china jug full of milk.

'The Society has been very concerned about this family since the mother died,' said Mr Sharpe. 'Very concerned.'

'That a society should be so concerned about its children is very commendable,' said Karla. 'Are you here to offer help?'

'Well, not in the way that I think you mean,' said Mr Sharpe. 'We are concerned about the *safety* of these children. We have been made aware that Patrick is in hospital due to falling off the back of a truck recently.'

'A most unlucky event,' Karla said. 'He and his little pal were being teased by two boys in their class – teased about their fathers being in the British Army. They were dared to show how brave they were by jumping on the back of a lorry.'

'The other boy's mother has made a statement in Store Street Garda Station,' I added.

'Those two boys had been teasing Patrick in school about his father for a long time,' said Karla. 'This was not the first time it happened.'

'The accident happened before you moved in, Miss Popper?' said Miss Spatt, taking out a little notebook from her briefcase.

'It did, Miss Spit,' said Karla.

'Spatt. My name is Spatt.'

'Sorry, Miss Spatt. I thought Nancy was doing a splendid job, but as she was working and looking after the little ones, and the mother was not long gone to her just reward, the family felt that I would be the ideal person to help out.'

'And do you not work yourself?' asked Mr Sharpe.

'I do. Nancy and I work at the same sewing establishment.'

'Then who is going to look after Patrick when he is convalescing?'

'Our boss at Mandel's has very kindly arranged for us to work different shifts as much as possible,' I said. 'And we have a special arrangement for when we're both at work at the same time. Tom, will you pop upstairs and get Mrs McGee?'

There was a pause in the conversation, during which time Miss Spatt walked around, inspecting first the kitchen, then Ma's room. She sat at the table and jotted down notes.

Mrs McGee followed Tom in.

'Good afternoon,' she said. 'We meet again.'

'That's right, that's right.' Mr Sharpe said this avoiding her eyes. He coughed, moved forward in the chair and sat very straight. 'We're in the process of establishing who is going to look after Patrick Kidd when he is discharged from hospital.'

'The odd time that the girls are both at work, it'll be me,' said Mrs McGee. 'I'm upstairs – directly above – and I'll be up and down keepin' an eye on the young fella.'

More notes were taken.

'What if the boy falls or there's an emergency?' Miss Spatt asked.

'Now the pair of yiz know these buildings. There isn't much happens that can't be heard in the other rooms. I'll be checkin' on him, but if there's an emergency, he'll know to shout and I'll come running down the stairs as fast as a greyhound to tend to him. If I'm out gettin' the messages, Mrs Perrin, next door to me, will keep an eye.'

Miss Spatt wrote some more notes in her notebook.

'If you don't mind me sayin',' Mrs McGee continued, 'I think Nancy's been doing a great job, and now she's her cousin come to stay, they'll be as right as rain.'

'Thank you, Mrs McGee,' said Mr Sharpe. 'That'll be all.'

Once she had closed the door, Mr Sharpe started again.

'We called into the school yesterday and noticed that you were absent three days last week, Thomas. What was the reason for that?'

I had a few seconds of panic as I knew that Tom had gone down the quays selling papers those mornings and would have been late for school by the time he got back. To avoid the beatings, he had mitched those days.

'I had to go to visit my little brother in hospital on those days, Mr Sharpe. Did the Master not tell you that?'

This much was true. Tom did visit Patrick on those days.

'Couldn't you have done that after school?' asked Miss Spatt coldly.

'Ah, he was so sick, Miss. He misses Ma and it was such a

long day 'til Nancy and Kate could go and visit him.'

'He was very sick,' I chimed in. 'That's why it was great that someone from the family could be with him. We didn't think missing a few days from school would matter.'

'Hmmm,' said Miss Spatt, writing in the notebook.

'And what about selling the newspapers?'

'Fully licensed,' said Tom, holding up the badge that was on the sideboard, paid for by selling Granny's mother-of-pearl rosary beads.

Mr Sharpe asked how much the rent was, and what money was coming in. Miss Spatt asked what we had for breakfast and what we were having for dinner. She asked about who came to visit us. She asked us where we got our clothes and shoes. Finally, she closed her notebook and put it back into her handbag.

'Well, that about covers it, Mr Sharpe,' she said.

'So?' asked Karla.

'What do you mean?' asked Miss Spatt, going out to the hall as Mr Sharpe held the door open for her.

'You are happy with what you see?' said Karla.

'We make a report to our superiors, not to the subjects of our investigation,' she said with a little sniff.

Karla stared at Miss Spatt without blinking. She looked as if she was trying to stop herself from passing a remark as she stood at the door. Once it was closed, she held up her finger to her mouth for us to be quiet.

We could hear Mr Sharpe speaking out in the hall: 'If I didn't know any better, I'd say they were expecting us.'

'I totally agree,' said Miss Spatt. 'But going on that visit, the Society doesn't have a case. I don't know what Gertrude Knaggs is talking about.'

We waited until the voices faded, and then we cheered for Karla and started singing 'Happy Days Are Here Again'. The back parlour hadn't seen such a happy day in a long time.

Chapter Twenty-Six

'Are you sure he said eight o'clock?' asked Lilly.

'I have no doubt about what time he said,' replied Karla. 'He said he might not be able to make it on time, but that we were to wait here.' She watched the faces carefully for any sign of Jacob, the moneylender, as we stood under Clery's clock.

Fianna Fáil was holding a big rally for Seán T. O'Kelly, the last before the election the following day. Like rivers flowing into the sea, local branches of the party from around the city were flowing into O'Connell Street. A big colourful banner from the Malahide branch passed by, with men and women marching behind it. A stage was set up at the pillars of the GPO where Éamon de Valera and other politicians would be speaking shortly to urge people to vote for O'Kelly.

'Are they Americans?' asked Lilly, as a group of soldiers in khaki uniform pushed through the crowd.

'Yes,' said Karla. 'Look at those smart caps they are wearing. I read in a magazine that they are called "garrison hats".'

'Ma said there's loads of them in town,' said Lilly. 'She saw them lining up to go to the pictures in the Metropole last night.' She leaned back against the window. 'Still no sign of

Jacob? I don't know why he couldn't have called to the house.'

'Because he is so busy and we need this money in a hurry,' said Karla.

'We're lucky he's able to help us out at such short notice,' I added. 'Who else could we have gone to?'

Lilly never answered. A brass band played in the distance. The music was coming from the direction of O'Connell Bridge. As it got louder, people started clapping and cheering.

'That's for the men who fought in Easter Week,' said a mother to her little son beside us. 'They're marching across the bridge and they'll be up on that stage in a few minutes.'

More people were pushing their way into O'Connell Street. Some lads had even climbed onto the roof of the air-raid shelter across from us in the middle of the street. I half wished we were up there ourselves, as the crowds started pressing us against the shop window of Clery's.

It was almost half-past eight. I was getting worried. If Jacob didn't arrive with the money, Charlie would have to hide somewhere in Dublin until we got it for him. He couldn't leave for England without money. And we all knew that once a boy escaped from Artane and stayed in the Dublin area, the police usually caught him within days.

'Karla!' shouted a voice.

A man wearing a flat cap with black curly hair peeping out from beneath it was waving in our direction.

Karla moved out to meet him and we followed. He pushed his way through the crowds to go around the corner into Sackville Place. When he reached Brooks Thomas's Hardware, he stopped.

'Which of you is Lilly?'

'I am,' said Lilly.

'If you don't mind, we can walk a little further and transact our business. It's a little quieter down here,' he said, pointing towards Earl Place.

Karla and I stood at one of the barred windows as they moved off. We could hear De Valera speaking back in O'Connell Street now. He was praising Seán T. O'Kelly.

'Is there anyone more appropriate for President, than a man who stood by Pádraig Pearse's side in 1916?' This was met by loud cheers and clapping.

Jacob had insisted on giving the money to Lilly, who would be the person to pay him back. As soon as they were finished their business, Lilly would give the money to me for Charlie.

'Finished,' said Lilly as she joined us outside the door of Brooks Thomas's. Jacob passed us with a quick 'Good evening, ladies.'

'Put that somewhere safe,' said Lilly, handing the envelope to me.

'Somewhere safe?' said a voice. We looked behind us. The voice was Mickser's. Beside him, with his hands in his pockets, stood a boy I didn't recognise. He was older than Mickser and a fighter from the look of his swollen jaw and cut lip.

'Wait a minute, girls, wasn't that Jacob Glickman?' he said.

'It is none of your concern who he is,' said Karla.

'She's right,' I said, sounding braver than I felt. 'It's none of your business.'

We kept walking.

'But it is our business,' said Mickser. 'Isn't it, Bulldog?'

'Without a doubt.' The voice was gravelly.

'C'mon girls,' said Lilly and our step quickened.

'Going home already?' Bulldog walked on the back of my shoes. We sped up. The boys kept close behind us. Sackville Place was deserted; everyone was at the rally.

'Leave us alone,' said Lilly. 'For God's sake, Mickser.' I could hear the quiver in her voice.

'Slow down. Anyone would think you're scared of us,' said Bulldog.

'Scared of the pair of you?' said Lilly with a forced laugh. 'What's the world comin' to?'

'It's comin' to this: you've been seen in the company of a moneylender and it so happens that we're in need of some money,' said Bulldog.

'If that's the case, see him yourself,' said Karla.

We were close to running when I heard somebody singing behind us. It was a song I recognised – 'Kevin Barry'. I turned around. A man walking on the footpath wasn't far behind the boys.

'Hey, Sconsie!' I shouted back at him.

'How are ya, Nancy?' he called back. He saw what was happening. 'Can I have a word, lads?'

Both boys turned around. We saw our chance.

'Run!' shouted Karla.

We took off, turning the corner into Marlborough Street. We ran past a woman pushing a pram, and past an old man walking a little black-and-white terrier. We didn't stop at North Earl Street. A man driving a horse and cart shouted at us that we'd be killed, but still we didn't stop. We were the lucky ones that Sconsie had arrived when he did and had given us a chance to run, but Lilly and I knew Mickser. He wouldn't give up. As fast as we were running, we were no match for the boys running after us. They were soon close behind us.

Past the pawnshop and Tyler's boot repairs, we ran. The boys were on our heels now. Around the corner of the second air-raid shelter, outside the Pro-Cathedral, Karla collided with a man coming in the opposite direction. She lost her balance and fell forward onto the street. Her knee was bleeding. We went to help her up, but the man was ahead of us, holding out his hand.

Another man came behind him. They were both wearing the khaki green uniform of the American army. Though we had seen some soldiers among the crowd at the rally, we hadn't for the life of us thought we'd ever get to speak to any.

'Pard' me, Ma'am,' said the man who had collided with Karla, pulling out a big white hankie and giving it to her. 'Are you okay?'

'Knee feels sore,' panted Karla, dabbing it with the hankie.

'Stop a minute and catch your breath,' he said. He glanced at Mickser and Bulldog. They had stopped running and were leaning against the air-raid shelter. 'Are those guys bothering you?'

'Yes,' Karla and I said together.

'They were running after us, trying to rob us,' said Lilly.

'Trying to rob you? No kidding? Chuck, can you have a *conversation* with those two young men, please?'

'Sure, Bernard,' he said, pronouncing it Bern*ard*.

Chuck walked towards Mickser and Bulldog. But there was no conversation to be had. He had hardly taken a step on the street when the two boys turned around and fled in the opposite direction.

'You leave those girls alone, y'all hear?' shouted Chuck after them. Four girls walking towards us stopped when they saw the uniforms, and stood on the steps a few houses down from the Pro-Cathedral, watching our every move.

'Hope you're comfortable enough to walk now,' said Bernard. 'Is your knee all right?'

'It will be all right, thank you very much,' said Karla.

'Our pleasure, Ma'am,' said Bernard.

'Have you ever been to Hollywood?' asked Lilly. The soldiers both laughed.

'No, Miss, neither of us has – not so far anyway. I'm from New York City,' said Bernard. 'Chuck is from Kansas.'

'We're both from Dublin, but Karla, our friend here, is from Prague,' said Lilly.

Bernard looked at Karla. 'From Prague to Dublin. I can only imagine what brought you here,' he said. His voice was soft, and I could see that Karla was trying to keep her strong-girl face.

'Thank you for the handkerchief and for helping me up,' she said. 'We really must go now.'

We marched past the girls on the steps, all standing with their mouths open. Lilly made the most of the moment by smiling as we passed – a smile that made it look as if we lucky ones were bestowing grace on these less fortunate creatures. A girl with brown-rimmed glasses made a face back at her. We walked on, ignoring them. After that, Karla paused and dabbed her knee a few times, but the bleeding had almost stopped.

Chapter Twenty-Seven

Although Mickser and Bulldog were gone, we were still keeping a close eye on who was around as we passed the row of red-brick houses beyond the Pro-Cathedral. Lilly almost walked into the post box on the footpath. Normally we would have laughed at this, but we weren't in the mood for seeing the funny side of things.

Something was amiss at Tobin's Bar. It was further down, on the far side, at the corner of Waterford Street. Shouts and whistles could be heard over the bikes, horses and carts, and the odd car that drove down Marlborough Street. Half a dozen boys were huddled around somebody. A barman stood like a guard dog at the door. Three or four girls perched on the low ledge below the shop window. We could now see that a woman was lying on the path.

A little white-and-tan terrier came around the corner, sniffing at the girls' shoes.

'Hey, Johnny! Watch this. Nobody make a move.'

The dog peered in the door of the bar but thought the better of entering. He sniffed his way through the boys and spotted the woman on the ground. Picking her foot as his target, he cocked his leg and did a pee. The boys and girls all laughed and cheered. I felt sickened. Imagine finding that funny!

Karla stopped on the footpath, said something in her own language and tore across the street. We followed.

'Proud of yourselves?' she shouted. 'You think this is a good way to treat old people?'

'We're only having a bit of fun, Miss,' said one of the boys.

'Fun? This is your idea of *fun?*' shouted Karla.

Nobody spoke for a moment. The dog continued on his way down towards Sean MacDermott Street.

'Well, if you don't like it, why don't you go back to where you came from?' said one of the girls. She put her hands on her hips and stared at Karla.

Karla stared back and said something in her own language. You didn't have to speak it to know what she was saying. The girl started moving away.

'Come on, folks, it looks like there isn't much *fun* here after all.' With a smirk on her lips, she turned the corner into Waterford Street. The other girls followed first, then the boys. Nobody looked us in the eye.

I looked at the woman on the ground.

'Oh my goodness, look who it is,' I said. Her cap had fallen off her and her coat was up above her knees. It was the Pig Farmer.

'Do any of you know this woman?' the barman asked.

'She lives over in Summerhill,' said Lilly.

'She came into the pub looking for her husband,' said the

barman. 'Said his name was Martin Knaggs.'

'Her husband?'

'That's right. Before I had a chance to say anything, she started shouting that he was hiding somewhere and she needed to talk to him about his niece,' said the barman. 'Then she stumbled out the door and fell on the pavement. I've sent one of the young lads 'round for the doctor. Would you mind staying with her for a few minutes?'

'Of course, we will stay. Would you have a coat or a blanket to put under her head?' asked Karla.

The barman went inside and one of the customers came out with an old coat and handed it to Karla.

'You lift her head and I'll slip it under,' said Karla.

It felt strange putting my hands on the Pig Farmer's head, but there was something about seeing her lying there on the street that made me feel sorry for her, in spite of all that had happened. I picked up her cap and pulled it onto her head. Her eyelids started opening. She sat up, faster than you'd say 'Curly Wee and Gussie Goose', and grabbed my arm.

'Jenny!'

'It's Nancy,' I said, remembering she had called me Jenny on Sunday.

'For heaven's sake, Jenny Knaggs, don't you think I'd know my husband's niece?'

'Mrs Knaggs—' I started.

'Don't Mrs Knaggs, me, Jenny. I might have known you'd run away from the laundry again. The nuns are driven astray with you. But I was looking for you to ask you a question. Why did you give the baby to *her*?'

'What baby?'

'What baby – do you hear her!'

'I don't know what you're talking about, Mrs Knaggs. I don't know anything about any baby—'

'Ah yes, pretend you don't know. I'm talking about *your* baby. The one your mother was trying to force *me* to take while you were in the laundry giving the poor nuns an awful time.'

'You're mixing me up with someone else.' But the Pig Farmer continued as if I hadn't spoken.

'Imagine asking *me* to take your baby. You a wayward young wan barely sixteen! Martin listened to my good advice, of course. Always a sensible man, my Martin.'

'Mrs Knaggs, you're—'

'Why did you give the baby to Honora Murphy? Did it to spite me, didn't you?'

'Are you talking about Granny?' I asked.

'Granny? Who's Granny? I'm talking about Honora Murphy. Haven't I lived next door to her for years?' She prodded me on the arm. 'I advised her against it. Told her she was asking for trouble taking *your* baby, but would she listen? Not at all. Said she didn't care where the baby came from. Ordered me out of the house.'

Aunt Gretta's letter floated back into my head. The story of the girl in the Magdalen Laundry … could there be truth in the Pig Farmer's words? Suddenly a tear trickled down her face.

'Anyway, I wouldn't take your baby because Martin and I thought we'd have our own little child. Five happy years we had together, but didn't he go and die in the war?' She slumped back onto the path and continued to talk as if she was thinking out loud. 'No Martin, no baby … in the end I was left with nobody.'

'There, there,' said Karla, rubbing the Pig Farmer's arm.

'You don't suppose …' started Lilly, but she stopped when the Pig Farmer sat upright again.

'What am I doing here?'

'Mrs Knaggs, you've had a fall,' I said as kindly as I could. 'I think you'd better stay where you are for a few minutes.'

'Good advice,' said a voice behind us. A man in a black suit knelt beside the Pig Farmer and opened his black leather bag.

'Lord above! Are you from Farrell's Funeral Undertakers? ... Am I dead?' asked Mrs Knaggs.

'Indeed, you're not dead,' said the man in the suit. 'I'm your doctor, Mrs Knaggs.'

'Doctor Carter?'

'You've gone back a bit there, Mrs Knaggs. Doctor Carter was in the practice all right, but he's retired now. I'm Doctor Wren.'

'I've had another of those—' We waited for her to finish the sentence, but the Pig Farmer stopped and slapped the doctor across the face. 'I want to go home!'

'*Please*, Mrs Knaggs,' said the doctor, putting his hands up in case she was going to hit him again.

The Pig Farmer sat on the footpath, a dazed look in her eyes. The doctor asked us if we had been there when she fell. Karla stepped forward and repeated what the barman had told us, and used fancy words such as 'delusions' and 'disorientated'. The doctor couldn't hide his surprise as he asked Karla a few more questions. He finished examining the Pig Farmer.

'Do any of you live near her?' he asked.

'I'm her next-door neighbour,' I said.

'That's helpful. Your name is?'

'Nancy Kidd.'

As I spoke, the Pig Farmer searched our faces.

'Merciful hour, what am I doing here?'

'I'm your doctor, Mrs Knaggs, and my car's over there. I can help you up to get into it.'

She kept her lips in a thin line but allowed the doctor to help her up. He linked her over to his car, a dusty black Fiat 6. Once the passenger door was closed, he spoke back to us.

'I'm driving her to Grangegorman. She's had too many of these episodes lately. Would you be able to bring in some clothes and personal items from home, Nancy?'

'This evening?'

'Tomorrow would be fine.'

The girls and I looked at each other.

'I'll get my sister to bring them tomorrow after school,' I said.

We watched the car drive off.

'The poor woman,' said Karla. 'I know she is not our favourite person, but life can be so hard for people with dementia. One of my grandmothers had it.'

'What on earth was all that about Jenny Knaggs?' asked Lilly. 'It sounded like she was talkin' about the girl in your aunt's letter.'

'I thought the same,' said Karla.

'I could hardly take in all she was sayin',' I said. 'If she's right, Ma's mother was that sixteen-year-old girl.'

'A niece of Martin Knaggs,' said Lilly.

'We are going to have to verify these facts,' said Karla. 'But remember, I said to you, Nancy, that there was something more to the dispute between those two ladies?'

'For heaven's sake, will you speak plain English?' said Lilly.

'Let's get Charlie out of Artane first,' I said before Karla attempted to repeat what she had said in 'plain English'. 'Then we can find out about the mysterious Jenny Knaggs.'

If the information was true, I was learning more about a grandmother I had only found out about a few weeks ago. First that shock and now this! But Karla was right. There was no point in wondering and puzzling over what we had heard. The facts had to be checked.

Chapter Twenty-Eight

The way Karla pinned my hair so tightly beneath my cap, I felt like it was nailed to my head. I stood in the kitchen, the shirt collar tight around my neck and the boots like lumps of rock tied to my feet.

'Greetings, Isaac,' I said to the tiny mirror nailed onto the wall beside the fireplace. Pulling the peak of my cap forward, I pinched some grains of soot from the grate and smudged the dirt onto my face to make my skin look more like a boy's, but Karla dipped a cloth in the bucket of water and rubbed it off.

'A Jewish merchant is not going to take on a scruffy boy,' she said, brushing some dust off the jacket with her hand. 'That's better.'

Neither of us had work that day as we had agreed to work on Saturday. Ten minutes later, Karla and I were standing outside Ryan's Grocery on Sean MacDermott Street, where we were to meet Levi. I held an old kitbag with the clothes and boots for Charlie. A delivery van pulled up.

'Meet Isaac,' said Karla.

'Pleased to meet you, Isaac,' Levi said, smiling. 'Your first task is to throw that bag of clothes into the back.'

I opened the back of the van and buried the bag under some of the bales of cotton. As soon as I sat up front, Karla gave the door a couple of raps to say goodbye, and off we went. Levi wore a cap and a tan coat. He looked ahead and never spoke a word until we were passing by the park at Fairview.

'Remember, follow what I do when we are unloading the goods.'

When we came to the Malahide Road, my stomach started to tighten, but I kept reminding myself that this was our one chance to save Charlie. We had to take it. Levi passed the front gate of the school and swung left up Kilmore Road. Within minutes, we were passing the lodge on our left-hand side as we drove through the open gates. The infirmary was beyond it. Showtime – we hoped.

'What are we bringin' in?' I asked.

'Sheets and pillowcases here and a couple of bales of cotton to the workshops.'

'But I thought the boys would make their own sheets and pillowcases?'

'They make most things, but sometimes my boss does special deals for his loyal customers and the Brothers can buy these very cheap.'

He pulled up the van and we both got out. Levi whistled a tune as he opened the back of the van and pulled out three parcels covered in brown paper. I took the other two and followed him into the infirmary.

Inside, the smell of Jeyes fluid was overpowering. Levi walked through an open door into a little office. A nurse, in a starched white uniform, looked up at us from her desk. She took off her glasses.

'Good morning. The pillowcases?' said Levi.

She never said a word but pointed with the arm of her glasses towards a table over by the wall. We piled our packages on top of it.

'We have to get the sheets next,' said Levi. We both peered into the back of the van, hoping to see some sign of Charlie under the bales of cotton, but there was nobody there. Levi pulled out the sheets order.

'Leave one bundle behind, to give us more time,' he whispered.

We walked slowly in with the bundles of sheets. This time, the nurse was writing something in a ledger and didn't look up. Levi took the docket out of his pocket and placed it on the table. She snatched it, stood up, walked over to the table as if it was painful for her to do so, and counted the sheets in the pile.

'You're short one,' she said. 'Not signing 'til all goods are delivered.'

'Sorry, I will send Isaac back with that one,' said Levi.

On our way back to the van, we met a boy. There was blood all over his jacket sleeve and trousers. He looked younger than

Tom and was crying, but in a way that you'd think he was sucking the tears in.

'The nurse is there in the office,' said Levi quietly.

As we walked out the door, avoiding the splodges of blood on the floor, a screech came from the infirmary.

'Get that mess out of my office. Go up into the ward immediately!'

We both went to the back of the van. Still no sign of Charlie.

'Make sure she signs the docket. Then give her the top copy.'

I brought the last bundle in. The nurse pressed her lips together, signed the docket and pushed it towards me. I took it up.

'My copy, please!' she snapped before I had a chance to tear it off. I never answered but slapped the top copy on the table. Once I was back at the van, I did another check for Charlie, but still no sign.

'We can wait for a minute to see if he will come. If not, we will have to drive on to the workshop.'

Levi pretended to check all the dockets. I thought I felt the van move slightly.

'Time to go. I will close the doors first.' Levi climbed out, moved something about in the back of the van, and hopped back into the driver's seat. He looked at me and smiled.

'Our extra passenger is on board,' he said. 'Let's get the delivery to the tailors' workshop over and get out of this place.'

We drove on past the farmyard. Two boys wearing wellies that were too big for them were wheeling wheelbarrows full of manure out of one of the sheds. The smell of the pigs reminded me of the Pig Farmer. What was it like for her to find herself in Grangegorman? But I pushed all thoughts of her out of my head. I had a task in hand and couldn't let my mind wander.

Ahead on the right was the chapel. An air of quietness and calm hung over the building. How different it looked from the way I was feeling at that moment. Fingers crossed, we'd all be safely out of the grounds of Artane in the next fifteen minutes, I told myself.

Screech! Levi had put on the brakes on the van. A man's voice was roaring: 'Stop! Stop!' One of the Brothers had come running out of the chapel. He was waving two long paddles of arms.

'God, what does he want?' I said. He was pounding the front of the van.

Levi pulled down the window and stuck his head out.

'I have a delivery to make to the tailors' workshop,' he said.

'Something's happened,' shouted the Christian Brother.

My mouth went dry.

'Can you run over to the house there, quick, and make a phone call?' he said, pointing to a building across the avenue.

Levi paused. 'Call? Call whom?'

'Call the doctor,' said the Christian Brother. He was panting and was hardly getting his words out.

'For yourself?' asked Levi.

'Not me. It's Brother Adams … in the chapel. I don't want to leave him on his own.'

'What happened?'

'He's collapsed.'

'Let me have a look,' said Levi, opening the door of the van.

'You? What on earth would you know?' asked the Brother.

'I am a medical student.'

The Brother seemed surprised. He looked at the van and then over at me. Levi jumped out.

'Isaac, come in with us. Might need help with him.' I got out and followed them towards the chapel door. 'When did it happen?'

'Between eleven and twelve. He insisted on walking down to vote, even though he was complaining of a headache. I saw him come up the avenue around eleven o'clock.'

Inside, he tore up the main aisle towards an altar, his sandals squeaking on the polished tiles. We followed close behind. He swung right. At the kneeler in front of the statue of Our Lady, Brother Adams had fallen sideways onto the floor. His face was whiter than his mop of white hair. The other Brother knelt down and spoke into his ear.

'Brother Adams, it's Luke. Luke Heaney.'

Levi felt his pulse. He pulled up one of Brother Adams's eyelids and looked at his eye. Then he felt his forehead.

'Forget about the doctor, Brother Heaney. This man needs to get to a hospital straight away,' he said.

'Will we call for an ambulance then?'

'Not enough time,' said Levi. 'Is there a car you could use to take him?'

'The only car we have is gone. Gone to a funeral down the country,' said Brother Heaney.

'Then *we* will have to bring him,' said Levi. 'Will you get one side of him and help me lift him? We'll have to do our best to carry him out. Isaac will open the door for us.'

Brother Adams was so small and thin that lifting him was easy. Between them, they carried him down the aisle and over to the door I held open. They were making their way out the door when two boys came running towards them.

'Brother Heaney,' said the taller one. 'Brother Briscoe said—'

'For God's sake, can't you see what—'

'He said Weaver never showed up for lunch duty,' blurted out the smaller boy.

Brother Heaney continued with the old Brother as if the two boys were invisible. They waited as he and Levi carried Brother Adams towards the van. The old Brother's eyelids started to flicker.

'Where are you taking me?' he muttered.

'We're bringing you to the hospital, Brother Adams. You fell in the chapel. Are you going to put him into the back?' Brother Heaney asked Levi.

'No. Too dangerous,' said Levi. 'If you sit in the front with him, beside me, Isaac can climb into the back. We will head for the Mater Hospital.'

Levi and Brother Heaney held onto Brother Adams while I held the door open. Then they lifted Brother Adams in and I closed the passenger door. The two boys stood watching us. The window on the driver's side was still open.

'That Charlie Weaver was trouble from day one,' Brother Heaney said, then he called out to the boys: 'Run back to Brother Briscoe and tell him to call the guards if Weaver is still missing. And make sure to tell him I've gone to the Mater with Brother Adams.'

Levi was at the back of the van, opening the door for me. 'Can't be helped,' he whispered.

Once in, the smell and dust of the flannel made my nose itchy, but as soon as the engine started up, I spoke to Charlie in the darkness.

'You all right, Charlie?'

'All right? With that brute in the front? I heard him: "Charlie Weaver was trouble from day one." I wish it was him that collapsed.'

'Look, we've to bring the old Brother to the Mater, but we

don't have to give up. You've changed your clothes?'

'I have. The old ones are in the bag now.'

'And the boots?'

'In the bag as well. Great to have my old newsboy boots back.'

'Here's the money we got from the moneylender yesterday.'

He put the envelope into his pocket.

'What'll I do when we get to the Mater?'

'Stay put until I get a chance to talk to Levi. There's still a chance that all of this will work.'

I sounded braver than I felt. Much braver.

Chapter Twenty-Nine

The doors of the van were flung open.

'We'll need you to open the doors, Isaac,' said Levi. I hopped out. 'Charlie, don't move until I come back,' he added in a whisper.

'This isn't the Mater,' I said, looking out.

'It is the Mater *Private*,' said Levi, heading around to the passenger door to open it for the Brothers. 'This is where the Brothers are treated.'

I ran up to the door between two pillars and found that it was slightly open. I pushed it in and held it as Levi and Brother Heaney lifted the old man out of the van and up the steps. Brother Heaney's face was red and sweaty. He was trying to copy Levi in the way that he was holding Brother Adams's arm and back. A nurse ran over as soon as she saw the Brothers in the hall. I felt a moment of panic. I knew her from visiting Patrick. She might recognise me. But I needn't have worried. All the attention was on Brother Adams.

'Nurse! We need a wheelchair straight away, please!' shouted Levi.

One was wheeled in almost immediately by two porters. They lifted Brother Adams into it.

'Tell Charlie we will go to the station after this,' Levi whispered in my ear before he took off down the corridor. 'Won't be long.'

I was about to go back to the van when three nuns out on the footpath turned towards the hospital door. I stood holding it open for them.

'We're here to see Sister Colmcille,' said the first nun to the nurse at the desk. The last nun took her time climbing the steps. It was Sister Olivia, a bunch of pink flowers in one hand.

I pulled my cap forward and kept my gaze towards the floor. If Sister Olivia recognised me, it could put not only Charlie and Levi in danger, but my whole family. How could I explain why I was helping Levi, dressed as a boy? It could undo everything we had planned and worked towards. She dropped a flower as she was crossing the threshold. I picked it up and handed it to her.

'Thank you, young man,' she said, blinking through her thick glasses. 'Can you hold the door for another wee minute? There are two more after me.'

I kept my head down.

'Probably has no English, Sister,' said the nurse at the desk to Sister Olivia. 'He came in with one of our foreign medical students who brought an emergency case. Sister Colmcille is up in Room 11.'

I kept looking down as if I hadn't understood what was said.

The last two nuns were walking very slowly towards the door. A phone rang at the desk and one of the nurses answered.

'They've just arrived. He's in good hands. That's grand. I'll give him the message,' she said. I could hear the shuffle of feet in the hall, and I looked up to see Mr Archer in a smart suit, standing in front of the desk.

'Is that message for me?' he asked.

'No, Mr Archer. It's for Brother Heaney. An escape from Artane. Brother Staunton wants to let him know that the guards have been informed.'

The last two nuns passed me and thanked me for holding the door. The first one had a walking stick and stopped, resting both hands on it.

'What was that?' she asked Mr Archer.

'One of those boys in Artane,' said Mr Archer. 'Gone and done a runner.'

'Poor Brother Staunton. What he has to put up with in that place,' said the second nun, whose breath was wheezy. 'It truly is a vocation to work with those ungrateful brats.'

Once she had passed me, I closed the door and slipped past the railings to the van. The street was quiet. I chanced opening the door into the back. Then I rooted among the fabrics as if I was looking for something.

'Nancy?' said Charlie. 'What's the plan now?'

'We're still going to the train station, but we need to be really careful. A call's just come to the hospital to let Brother Heaney know that the guards have been told about your escape.'

'They don't waste much time.'

'Give me that bag of clothes. I'll bring it up front with me so that I'll be ready to hop out at the train station. Here's Levi. Have to close the door now.'

* * *

By two o'clock, Levi and I were in the van coming towards Amiens Street Station. A garda on duty was stopping traffic coming into town from the Artane direction. Another was standing on the footpath at the entrance to the station, where we planned to pull up to deliver the parcel.

'What'll we do?' I asked Levi. My sweaty hands held onto the kitbag of clothes on my lap.

'Remember, we are just delivering a parcel to the station,' said Levi. 'I don't know if the girls will still be here. I will engage the guard in conversation. You open the back of the van to get the parcel and let Charlie out. Tell him to make sure to walk, not run. Remember, he's not in an Artane uniform, so once he is walking down the street like any ordinary boy, he should be fine.'

'I'll bring the parcel to the counter inside,' I said.

'Correct. Let's go.'

I jumped out and opened the door at the back. I rooted among the fabrics and took out the parcel that was to be left at the station. My hands were shaking as I put it under one arm. I had the kitbag of Artane clothes and boots in my other hand.

'Walk, don't run,' I whispered.

Charlie hopped out. Spotting a group of dockers coming towards us, he fell in behind them as if he had been with them all morning.

I overheard the guard talking to Levi.

'One of the old Brothers out in Artane had to be brought off to hospital – passed out in the chapel, we were told – and you can be sure one of the young ruffians out there took advantage of the fuss to do a runner.'

I stepped onto the footpath and felt someone brush against me. Mona scurried past, with Lilly close on her high heels. Neither girl looked at me. Lilly caught up with Mona and tapped her on the shoulder.

'I've a bone to pick with you, Miss.'

'Get your hands off me,' shouted Mona.

'I'll get my hands off you if you get your hands off my boyfriend,' shouted Lilly back.

'Ex-boyfriend. Barney Hogan's *my* boyfriend now.'

'I know what's been going on. He told me he was workin' late last night. But what's really happenin' is that YOU've been workin' on *him* to get *him* away from *me*.'

'This pair looks like trouble,' said the guard to Levi.

'Yes,' said Levi. 'Especially that one in the red hat.'

'Now, girls, *please,*' said the guard.

'This row is *beyond* the law,' said Mona, holding up her hand to stop the policeman.

'Not if you two are obstructing the peace,' said the guard.

Levi drove off in the van and I made my way to the steps going into the station. I checked to see if Charlie was still in view. There he was, walking past the North Star Hotel, hands in his pockets, his shaven head beneath a new cap, as usual pulled sideways. He strolled along the street as if he hadn't a care in the world. *Please get to Hairy Bacon's safely*, I thought.

I was relieved we had got this far in the plan, but part of me felt miserable. Charlie would be gone for ages; a sad and lonely time stretched ahead for me. He had walked away and I never wished him luck. I never even said goodbye.

I dumped the boots in a bin, and the Artane clothes were a heap of ashes in our grate before Tom or Kate got home that evening. I had put on a pot of spuds to boil when I heard someone banging on our door.

'Nancy Kidd! Nancy Kidd!'

I put my head out. Hairy Bacon's oldest son, Bill, was standing in the hall.

'Da told me to tell you the goods are on the ship.'

'Good lad,' I said. 'Tell him "thanks" from me!'

Chapter Thirty

Maggie was alarmed to find two policemen waiting at her door on Thursday evening when she got back from voting. When they told her that Charlie had escaped, she thought at first that it was some sort of joke. Then she saw that they were serious. She told them truthfully that she didn't know anything about where Charlie could be, and waited for the worst to happen.

'I couldn't believe it, Nancy,' she told me when she and Lilly called over on Sunday after Mass. 'One of them was near retirement and the other was startin' out. They came in, had a poke around, hardly asked me anything, and went on their way.'

'Probably afraid of you, Ma,' said Lilly, winking at me.

'And to think my own sister was in on it and I hadn't a clue,' said Maggie. 'And there I was looking for Charlie's boots that morning for a lad startin' on the readers this weekend. Couldn't figure out what I'd done with them.'

'Where's Karla?' asked Lilly.

'The Rosenbergs sent for her yesterday. The Rabbi got a message for her to contact the Red Cross in Prague,' I said. 'She was told to come prepared to stay the night.'

'I hope it's good news,' said Maggie. 'I'll call over again to thank her for all the help. Still can't believe Charlie did a runner and managed to get on the boat for England without bein' caught. And I'm still findin' it hard to believe that the Pig Farmer's no longer in there when I pass by her door in the hall.'

'Where's Kate today?' asked Lilly.

'Remember when I asked her to go to Grangegorman with the Pig Farmer's belongings? She said it meant the world to have her things brought to her. Didn't she beg Kate to come and visit her again? And Kate being Kate said she would. She's with her now.'

'Ah, Kate was always a kind girl,' said Maggie. 'It's more than that woman deserves, if you ask me.'

'What's the latest news on Patrick?' asked Lilly.

'The doctors think he'll be able to come home in two weeks,' I said. 'I'm heading in to see him this afternoon.'

'I'll try to get in to see him this week,' said Lilly, standing up. 'We've to go now, Nancy. Mona's keepin' an eye on Imelda and the twins.'

Maggie stood up and hugged me. 'Thanks again, love. Your mother would be proud of what you did. Tell Karla we'll call over to see her, tomorrow.'

* * *

After visiting Patrick in the afternoon, I sat down in the kitchen on my own. Kate and I had come across an old photo that morning, and it was now propped up by the milk jug. I had planned to show it to Maggie and Lilly, and yet I didn't feel the time was right when they were over. Something about the little picture made me want to get used to it and think about it before I shared it with them. *Maybe tomorrow when they come over* … I put the photo carefully back into the envelope and into the drawer of the dresser. As I pushed the drawer in, I heard Sconsie's voice out in the hall.

'Ah, that's wonderful, Miss. Wonderful altogether.'

Karla burst in. I hadn't a chance to stand up. She came over and grabbed both my hands.

'Mama and Vera have been found,' she said, laughing, and with that, she dropped my hands, sat down on the chair across from me, put her head down on the table and burst into tears.

'Aren't you happy?' I asked, confused.

She lifted her head. 'I *am* happy. I'm thrilled and relieved. But out of all of my aunts, uncles and cousins, none have survived. All those good people wiped out! And to die the way they did.'

She got up, took a cup, filled it with water from the bucket, and sipped from it.

'I've been holding back those tears for so, so long. Trying to keep hopeful but dreading what I might hear in the end. The good news about Mama and Vera is what I dreamed of, but for every happy feeling that I have in my heart right now, I have many sad ones for all the people who are gone.'

'And what about your mother and Vera? Where did they go after April?' I asked.

'On that date, a former colleague of Papa's was part of a group of doctors who visited Terezín. He spotted Mama and Vera and saw how ill they were. Thanks to him, they were transferred to a hospital the following day. What he did not know was that in the hospital, Mama changed our surname from the German-sounding "Popper" to "Pojar". That's why it was so hard to find them.'

'And how are they now?'

'Still weak, but getting better. So, my dear Nancy, I won't be staying too long with you. I am planning to return to Prague next week.'

'We were glad to have you!' I said, trying to hold back the tears that were gathering in my own eyes.

'Will you be watched again by the Cruelty Men when I am gone?' she asked, as if suddenly remembering why she was there. 'I was supposed to be a guardian and now I cannot see that through.'

'I've a feeling we won't be of concern after that last visit, Karla. They don't even have our neighbour to spy for them anymore.'

'The Pig Farmer! Did Kate go out today as planned?'

'She did, and take note: Kate insists that we all call her Mrs Knaggs now.'

'So, she is no longer the Pig Farmer! And what about the pigs?'

'They're being sold and the Corporation isn't allowing any more piggeries here. There's a new family movin' in at the end of the month. But speaking of Mrs Knaggs, there's something I want to show you.'

I took the envelope out of the drawer of the dresser and handed it to Karla.

'I came across a little album of photos in the Pig Farmer's kitchen — I mean Mrs Knaggs's kitchen — and I gave it to Kate to bring in to her. She was delighted to get her things, all except the little album. The very sight of it upset her. She asked Kate to get rid of it, but we took it out this morning to look through it and came across this photo.'

Karla took out the photo, stared at it and looked at me.

'What on earth was she doing with a photograph of you?' she asked. 'I must say it's a beautiful portrait, but why are you wearing such old-fashioned clothes in it?'

'It's not me. Look at the name on the back.'

'Jennifer Knaggs,' Karla read aloud. 'My goodness, all the talk that day about Jenny Knaggs. Was it all true? The resemblance is remarkable.'

'If this photo is anything to go by, it is. We're hoping to find out more about Jennifer Knaggs.'

'Are you going to ask at the Magdalen Laundry?'

'We thought we'd try Grangegorman Hospital first. Remember Aunt Gretta's letter? She said that's where our grandmother died.'

'What an astonishing turn of events,' said Karla. 'You may find out about family members you never knew existed.'

'Maggie and Lilly were here this morning and were asking 'specially for you,' I said, suddenly remembering. 'I didn't show them the photo – we had only found it this morning – but I will take it out when they come back tomorrow. What about Levi? You were to meet him in Rosenbergs?'

'Sadly, he found out that both his parents were transferred from Terezín to Auschwitz last October. Like so many of our people, they did not survive. Levi's father, Reuben, was a good friend of my father's – they worked together – so I am sad on that account, too. They died the same way as my aunts, uncles and cousins. It was one of the hardest tasks I ever faced to tell him my good news when he had to face such awful news of his own.'

'Poor Levi! What's he going to do?'

'He is going back to London to finish his course,' said Karla.

'You'll stay in touch, though?'

'In touch?' said Karla.

'I mean, write to each other?'

'We will write, for sure. We have been friends for so long, after all.'

'*Friends*? Isn't he – well – your boyfriend?'

'Levi? Boyfriend? No, he is not my boyfriend. What gave you that idea?'

'The way you met him and talked about him. I thought it was on account of loving you that he helped Charlie escape.'

'Ah, yes. Levi wanted to help Charlie, but he also wanted to pay me back for what my family did for him. You see, my mother helped Levi escape from Prague and go to London. Once he made it safely there, my father's old friend – a doctor in St Bart's – looked after him.'

'But don't you love him?'

'I do like him, but not in the boyfriend–girlfriend way. When I felt low, he helped me and I did the same for him. We each knew what the other was going through, but it was never a romance.'

'But he's so handsome!' I said, baffled that I was so wrong.

'He is very handsome, I agree. But how can I put this…? He's more like a big brother. Levi and I *will* write to each other,' she said, patting her hair and sitting up straight. 'He is a good friend, like you, Nancy. I know I'm not leaving for another week, but I am telling you now that I hope *we* will write too.'

'We will but I'm goin' to miss you at work,' I said. 'And at home!'

'And I'll miss the conversations, the walks, and of course the singing!'

* * *

By the last Friday in June, Karla had left. I had been moved to the sewing machines in Mandel's, thanks to Miss Curran who asked me to fill in for one of the machinists one day and liked my work. It looked likely that I was going to be asked to stay on permanently. By that Friday, Patrick was also well enough to leave the hospital. The McGees, the Perrins, Sconsie and other neighbours all stood out at the door to welcome him home. The warm weather had everyone in good humour. There were cheers and clapping as Patrick made his way into the hall. I stopped him before he opened the door into our place.

'Karla's gone. She was sorry to miss you, but she left a present for you.' He hobbled in on crutches, and as soon as he was in the door, a little black pup jumped up on him.

'Meet Lenni,' said Tom. Patrick sat down on a chair and the pup jumped up on his lap, trying to lick his face.

'At last, my own dog!' said Patrick, and he laughed as the pup tried to chew the wooden crutch.

'See the little collar on him? That came from Sister Olivia,' said Kate. 'There's a letter for you, Nancy,' she went on, pointing to a white envelope on the table. I tore it open.

20 Kingsgate Road
Kilburn
London
24 June 1945

Dear Nancy,

You heard I made it. I'm working with my uncle on the buildings. I am glad or should I say very happy to be gone from you know where. Thanks to yourself and L. for the lift into town that day.

Would you believe I met a lad last week who did the same as me in 1941 and who do you think helped him only H.B.! He says the same man has helped half a dozen boys or more to get to England over the years.

I miss Ma and the girls but I've a good landlady and the money is better than the papers.

I also miss the oldest of the Kidds of Summerhill and if she wrote to me, I'd write back.

Your friend,
Charlie Weaver

And the oldest of the Kidds of Summerhill decided that she would write. And Charlie wrote back!

A group of young people on Waterford Street, Dublin, in the 1940s. Photo courtesy of the McAuley family.

HISTORICAL THEMES

Housing

All of the main characters in this book are fictitious but they were inspired by the history of north inner-city Dublin. Readers may find it surprising that Nancy and the Pig Farmer lived in rooms with grand titles like 'front parlour' and 'back parlour'. To find out why, we need to go back to the eighteenth century when the houses were built. In those days, the Irish Parliament met in Dublin, and Members of Parliament and their families needed to have a house in town. If you walked along Summerhill at this time, you would have seen a street of grand Georgian houses. The first change came about at the end of the eighteenth century when the southside became more fashionable to live in. Then the passing of the Act of Union (1801) meant that the Irish Parliament no longer met in Dublin. Members of Parliament now had to travel to London, and their families and friends no longer needed houses in Dublin.

From 1800 to 1840, Summerhill became an area where solicitors and doctors lived and had their offices. But the Great Famine in the 1840s brought further change to the area. Huge numbers of poor people from the country drifted towards Dublin. By the 1860s, these big houses – originally built for one family – were being split up and rented out to several families. By 1911, the Dublin tenements were described as the worst slums in Europe. Houses were overcrowded, in some cases with families of ten children or more living in one room. There was no electricity or running water – people got their water from a tap in the yard – and one outdoor toilet was shared by all the families living in the house.

In the overcrowded tenements, many people caught tuberculosis, or T.B. The hospital that Esther Kidd was supposed to go to on Pigeon Road, Ringsend, was one of the hospitals set up for treating patients with T.B.

In the 1920s and 1930s, some families were moved from the inner city to suburbs such as Marino, Cabra and Crumlin, but during the Second World War, referred to in Ireland as 'the Emergency', a shortage of both building materials and builders meant that many of the building projects were put on hold.

Industrial Schools and Magdalen Laundries

Industrial schools, such as Artane and Goldenbridge, played an important part of life in Ireland at the time, especially for the people of the inner city. In 1950, there were fifty-one industrial schools in the country, all run by nuns, brothers or priests. Children could be brought to court by the National Society for the Prevention of Cruelty to Children ('the Cruelty Men'), the school attendance officer, the Society of St Vincent de Paul, the Garda Síochána (police) and the Legion of Mary. Why were children then sent to institutions? The most common reasons were: both parents or one parent had died; a child was found begging; a child had missed too much school; or a child had been found guilty of petty crimes such as shoplifting.

The Magdalen Laundry in the story was one of ten laundries in the twenty-six counties of Ireland. The main reason girls ended up in such places was because they were pregnant and not married. They were sent there by people ranging from their family to the local police. They worked in the laundry for no pay. In some instances, girls were transferred to laundries from industrial schools. The Magdalen Laundry in Sean MacDermott Street was the last one to close, in 1996.

Employment

The factory Nancy worked in is fictitious, but there were clothing factories in Foley Street in the 1940s, such as Dinkiewear and Liberty Gowns. The Abbey Clothing Company in nearby Abbey Street was another clothing factory in the area, and Todd, Burns & Co. in Mary Street, where Nancy bought the remnant of fabric in the first chapter, also had its own readymade clothing factory. It was mostly women who were employed in these factories, and in the commercial laundries, such as the Phoenix Laundry in Russell Street, where Mona worked. Workers there were among the 1,500 members of the Irish Women Workers' Union to go on strike in 1945, demanding two weeks' paid holidays. Led by Louie Bennett and Helen Chenevix, their demands were met by the laundry owners. This victory wasn't included in this novel as it happened after the story finished. Mitchell's Rosary Beads Factory, where Maggie and Lilly worked, was situated in Waterford Street, a street that no longer exists.

The newsboys selling newspapers on the street were a common sight and sound in Dublin in the 1940s. It is true that they required a badge to work and that there was a garda (policeman) whose job it was to check on this.

Mrs Hanlon who sold flowers in the street and her sister who collected and sold second-hand clothes represent the street-sellers who lived in the community. Her husband was a docker, and many dockers lived in the area where the story was set. They worked at unloading goods from ships. It was a hard life and the work was never guaranteed. Every morning, dockers had to go to a particular spot for a 'read'. There, a man known as a stevedore called out names for work that day. A docker got work only if he heard his name called out. It was common for the dockers to be given nicknames, hence the name 'Hairy Bacon' was given to the docker who helped Charlie escape.

Kindertransport

When the German army marched into Czech lands in March 1939, thousands of Jewish people's lives were at risk. While Karla is a fictional character in this novel, Nicholas Winton, the man who brought children, most of them Jewish, from Prague to London on a Kindertransport, was a real person. This young English stockbroker organised the rescue of 669 Czech children in 1939. He made arrangements not only for their journey to England, but also for homes where they could stay once they arrived. I have not been able to prove that any of the children he rescued came to Ireland from England, although 370 of them have never been traced. However, a small number of children did arrive in Ireland through other Kindertransports.

Terezín or Theresienstadt

Terezín, a camp-ghetto northwest of Prague, was established in 1941 for Jews from Prague and other parts of German-occupied Bohemia and Moravia. One of the reasons why the Nazis set it up was to house famous, elderly and privileged Jews, not only Czechs but also Germans, Austrians and citizens of other countries in western Europe. For propaganda purposes, it was put forward as a 'model camp'. The Red Cross was even permitted to check on the camp in June 1944. A completely false picture of the place was painted for this visit; some of the inmates had been deported to other concentration camps, such as Auschwitz, to make it look as if the people in Terezín had lots of space. Houses were painted. Fake cafés and shops were built. Once the visitors were gone, everything went back to the way it had been.

Of the 144,000 Jews sent to Terezín, almost one in four died there. Approximately 88,000 were transferred to Auschwitz and other death camps.

Also from The O'Brien Press

The Sound of Freedom

Ann Murtagh

It's spring 1919, and Ireland's War of Independence has broken out. In a cottage in County Westmeath, thirteen-year-old Colm Conneely longs to join the local Volunteers, the 'Rainbow Chasers' who are fighting for an Ireland free from English rule. But Colm has another ambition too – to make a new life in America, working as a fiddle player and involved in the republican movement there.

When spirited Belfast girl Alice McCluskey – who speaks Irish, shares his love of Irish music and is also committed to 'the cause' – arrives in town, Colm's dreams take a new turn. Where will his talent lead him? And how will a long-held family secret shape his future?

'Action-packed … I just couldn't put it down.'
– *Ireland's Own*

'[A] well-crafted tale not only bringing Irish history to a new generation but entwining readers young and not-so young in a web of intrigue and family secrets.' – *Evening Echo*